It's Just a
Mickey Situation

Drucilla Hawkins

PAGE PUBLISHING, INC.
Conneaut Lake, PA

First originally published by Page Publishing 2020

ISBN 978-1-6624-0076-6 (pbk)
ISBN 978-1-6624-0077-3 (digital)

Printed in the United States of America

Prologue

Being hog-tied, blindfolded, gagged, and dragged out my house had me scared as fuck. I don't know where I am or who kidnapped me. They threw me into an icy cold room made of concrete floors and walls, and then they beat me senseless. I sat alone in the dark, bound to a chair. I could barely breathe. I went into panic mode as soon as I came to. I shook my head back and forth, straining against the tight bindings, trying to unrope myself but to no avail. I was still tied down to that fucking seat. I gave up and sobbed quietly.

I sat there, forever thinking, *Who could've been out to get at me in such a way?* The more possibilities I ran down, the more confused I became. I no longer had Larnell because he was gone, and li'l Micheal was with my best friend, who'd left my house just an hour before I'd been kidnapped.

Then I heard what sounded like a door opened and closed. I heard someone walking toward me in heels, and sweat beads started dripping down the back of my neck. The person clad in heels stood in front of me for what felt like forever before speaking or moving. She then slapped me across the face and snatched off the blindfold. I blinked rapidly, willing my eyes to adjust to the dimness of the room, but I still couldn't make out anything but a figure. I tried mumbling something, a protest, anything, but it all came out as nonsense through the gag. Then she spoke. She had the voice of my best friend, and that's how I knew I was about to die.

"So, you, grimy bitch, I bet you didn't know I knew it was you who set me up and tried to ruin me."

Chapter 1

A year prior…

I sat on my bed, twisting my hair around my finger, waiting on Janikka to pick up her phone. Larnell walked into the house screaming.

"Where you at, Anita!? I'm hungry!" I rolled my eyes and closed my phone.

I am Anita Jones, mother of one. I'm twenty-seven years old. I have a sexy-ass caramel complexion, I stand at about 5'5" with the bra size of 38C and waist size at a ¹¹⁄₁₂. In short, I'm a bad bitch with a sorry-ass nigga straight drop.

"I'm in the room, here I come in a minute, baby!"

I've been with Larnell going on two years now. I met him through my best friend Janikka's girlfriend, Darnisha, one night at a club and been with him ever since. He was a fine piece of specimen when I first laid eyes on him, looking like a dark-skinned version of Terrence Howard when he played in *The Best Man*. He had Hershey-chocolate smooth skin, a goatee around his mouth with a hint of gray at thirty-five years old, he's 6'1" and 280 pounds. I was in love at first sight, and he was dressed to kill that night in some black slacks, a crisp, white button up, a diamond stud in his left ear, some fresh Stacy Adams out the box, and he had intoxicated me with one of my favorite men cologne by Ralph Lauren called Polo Blue. I was happy of our first year in the relationship, but this past year has been long difficult and very unhappy. Hearing my name snapped me out of my thoughts.

"Anita! Anita, bitch, you know you fucking hear me calling your stupid ass. I'm not gonna tell you again that I'm hungry!"

As soon as I walked into the living room, I stepped into the palm of Larnell's hand.

"Bitch, what took you so long to answer? Was you on the phone again? Huh?"

"No."

"Then what took you so long? I was calling your name for five minutes."

"I was taking the clothes out the closet that I'm going to be wearing tonight when me and Janikka go see our client."

"Whatever, Anita, I'm hungry, and I don't have time for your shit today, so go fix me something to eat before I get frustrated than I already am, and it won't be a good look for you."

"Yes, Larnell, do you want anything in particular for lunch today?"

"No, but hurry the fuck up."

So that's how me and Larnell's relationship started turning into after I found out he was on drugs. I'm not talking weed, I'm talking about that heavy-shit crack to be exact. I remember just pulling an all-nighter with Jay, dealing with a client. It was around 6:30 a.m., and I was dog-tired, all I wanted to do was shower and lay down because I had to take li'l Micheal to school at 8:00 a.m. I walked in the room but didn't see Larnell in the bed and heard the shower running; assuming that he was getting ready for work, I walked in the bathroom and had to do a double take when I saw Larnell pullin' on the glass dick sitting on my toilet in his boxers. He didn't even stop, he just looked at me and kept on pulling. I slapped that shit out of his hand without thinking, and he slapped my face just as hard. That's when the hitting began, and that's when I found out that Larnell didn't have a job and never did. He will wake up at six every morning, go in the bathroom, start the shower, and get high, but by then I was too far gone about how long it's been going on and what else he had been lying about. My relationship with Larnell hadn't been the same since.

"Here you go, Larnell. I'm about to go shower, call Jay, and get dressed for our client. Do you need anything else before I go?"

"Naw, I'm good, just don't be gone with that bitch all day and night."

I walked in the back room seething hot, looking for a blunt or something to calm me down. I hated when he referred my best friend, Janikka, as bitch because if it wasn't for her, I wouldn't never met Larnell. I love Janikka, she's the sweetest person I have ever known. We've been best friends for six years now. I met Janikka during her freshman year in college at UCLA. I was a junior then, but it was something about her that screamed freedom because I had none. I was with Micheal, li'l Micheal's dad for about two years then and was more locked down with him than I was with my own parents. I was only allowed to go to school and work. Then when I got pregnant my senior year, I had to leave school, but Jay never stopped loving me because I thought I was head over heels in love. That's what made me love her so much more in return. She was the one I ran to when Micheal cheated on me and didn't come home sometimes while I was pregnant and alone. It was also Janikka who helped me leave his ass when I felt that I couldn't take it no more. After six years of an unhealthy relationship with my baby's daddy, two years later, here I am in another one. As I say there on my bed, lit my blunt up and blazed before I took my shower, I called Janikka again.

"Hello?" Janikka said.

"Hey, baby, wassup? I called you earlier, but you didn't answer, we still on for later?"

"Yea, we still on. I was arguing with Darnisha ass again over some bullshit when you called, so I didn't click over, but wassup with you, sweetheart, what you doing?"

"Shit, nothing, girl, just getting ready to get in the shower and dealing with Larnell broke ass again."

"Nene, baby, I don't know why you deal with his shit, you deserve so much better."

"I know, I know, Jay, but I love him, and li'l Micheal loves him, so I deal with his shit."

We went back and forth for a minute about Larnell before I hung up the phone. I put my blunt out and hopped in the shower before it was time for me to go.

Chapter 2

While I was getting ready to leave to go meet up with Anita, Darnisha called me to apologize again for these ridiculous accusations she kept throwing my way. I've been with Darnisha for almost three years now, and she's still thinking that I'm fooling around on her. I hated dealing with Darnisha's bullshit before I go see a client because then I can't give my client my all, and in my line of business, you make sure you give it your all. I've been working with clients for three years now, and everything's been running smoothly. I had my own duplex house in Signal Hills, overlooking the city of Long Beach. I had my ownership pink slip papers of two cars, which was a mini Benz, and a Ford Focus that I paid car notes on just so it could look good to the IRS. I owned a beauty shop called JAY'S ALL-PURPOSE BEAUTY SHOP with a slogan that says, "If you need it, we weave it." I'll say that I'm doing quite well at the age of twenty-five years old with BA in business and an AA in accounting.

I could've been working in somebody corporate's firm, but that's not my get down. I'm self-employed, and I'm my own boss. I thought that everything was solid, including my weird love life until I met Darnisha Hall. The day I walked into HBM Law Offices on Crenshaw and Manchester right next to the Social Security Office, I literally stopped in my tracks when I saw her sitting behind the receptionist desk talking on the phone. She had the most addictive deep brown eyes I ever saw. When she looked at me, she hung up the phone.

She walked from behind the desk, and my breath got caught in my throat. She was dark chocolate with smooth skin, she had 34D cups sitting nice and perky in her silk blouse, her hair was shoulder length, all black and straight down with a gold clip. She looked like she weighed about 160 pounds to go with her 5'7" height. She had the prettiest lips, and when I looked down at her toes, they were freshly pedicured and polished. When I saw her, I would have been starstruck because she could've passed for Gabrielle Union's twin. Just a little bit darker. She had the height and all. So in short, I sized up and fell in love. I was so occupied undressing her with my eyes I didn't hear her saying.

"Hello, miss. Miss, may I help you?"

"Oh yes, I'm here to meet with a Mr. Hall."

She sashayed back behind the desk, and my eyes went directly to her ass, and what an ass that was. All nice and perfectly round.

"Your name, please?"

"Janikka Williams."

"Yes, here you are. Mr. Hall is expecting you."

I was there because my financial advisor thought that I needed a lawyer and felt Richard Hall was the best man for the job. Every time I see Mark Lewis, I thanked him. After the meeting, I walked back to the receptionist desk, cleared my throat, and asked the beautiful woman what her name was. She reached out some feminine hands to wrap around mine and said, "I'm Darnisha Hall. Ms. Williams, is there anything else I can do for you today?" She tried hard not to show that she was eyeing me up and down in my Donna Karan pinstripe, with a hot pink blouse underneath, with some dark pink pointed heels and silver accessories.

"Yes, you can help me, Darnisha, but it's something we'll have to discuss at dinner. What time do you get off?"

She looked shocked from me being so forward, but said, "Eight o'clock tonight."

I told her that I'll see her then and walked out the office. Shit we've been together ever since!

"Darnisha, you need to stop with this bullshit. I told you already over and over again I'm not fucking cheating, and I'm not fucking Toya!"

"I know, baby, but I be having flashes sometimes when I sit at work, and you don't answer your phone. I'm sorry."

"Sweetheart, I was in the shower, I'm heading out the door right now to meet Anita because we have a client to take care of tonight."

"Oh, all right, baby! So Imma call you later to check on you. Be careful! I love you."

"I love you too, Darnisha! But don't call, Imma have my phone off, I'll call you when I'm done."

I hung up the phone so she wouldn't complain because I knew it was coming. I clicked my unlock button to the Ford, I only use it for business and jumped in the car. I put my li'l Webbie *Savage Life Pt.1* CD in the player, put it on number six, started the ignition, and pulled off bouncing my head to "Gutta Bitch," going to go pick up my gutta bitch Anita. I'm just thinking about how far we've come since we started this business with the clients. I'm glad that I chose a thorough bitch like her to be by my side when I deal with these clients. Lately, she'd been trippin' though. I can't pinpoint what the problem is. But I sure have been watching her very closely. It's crazy how some people get greedy when they're already eating lovely. I think it had something to do with that no good nigga Larnell she's with. Then again, maybe I'm trippin', but I don't care how long we've been friends, I trust no one and suspect all!

I pulled up to Anita's house forty-five minutes later. She lived in the upper-class side of Los Angeles in Baldwin Hills on Stocker and Victoria Lane. It's nice up here on the hills, but I preferred Long Beach, the city by the sea! I parked next to her BMW on her spacious driveway. Anita got one of them one-story brownstone houses with dark green grass growing on her front lawn. It's a beautiful layout, but the inside was no comparison. She lived in a two-bedroom, two-bathroom house, a patio with a backyard, a living room, and a dining room right next to the kitchen. Her kitchen was laid out with stainless steel everywhere, from the stove to her cooking appliances. I remembered when we went to buy her refrigerator and dishwashing machine. Her dining set table was a seater for four, a nice, black wooden table. The living room furniture was pushed out with black-and-cream leather couches. A 42-inch plasma screen TV was connected to some speakers that make a movie turn into surround sound at the movie theater. A recliner chair that's all black and leather. A cream wooden table with coasters for li'l Micheal.

Then she got li'l Micheal's room decked out in Spider-Man style. Li'l Micheal loved Spider-Man, so, of course, on his twin bed, his comforter was Spider-Man. His closet was spacious enough to fit a TV and stand in there with clothes. He had his own TV on a stand for his Wii, iBox, DVDs, and whatever else he decided to do with it. He had a blue-and-red dresser drawer full of under Ts and underwear. Two little beanie bags that's blue and red. Li'l Micheal is spoiled. I must say that my girl spent money and time decorating her home, and it's always a pleasure entering her house.

I got out the car, went to the door, and knocked three times. Larnell opened the door, greeted me, and walked back to the couch. All I was thinking was *You bum-ass, lazy-ass nigga*, but I wouldn't dare say it aloud because Nene would down my throat! Just as I was thinking that, she walked out the back room.

"Hey, girl, when you get here?" she asked.

"Shit not too long ago, probably about three minutes." I laughed.

"You stupid, hold on, I'm almost ready. Larnell, can you come back here with me for a minute?"

Larnell looked back at her and said, "Yea, baby, here I come!"

When Larnell went to the back room, they closed the door, but my nose ass went to go listen. Maybe it was me being suspicious, but I went anyways. I heard Nene saying, "Is this okay to wear right now when I go see my client?"

I guess he looked her up and down because it took a minute for him to say, "Yea, you look all right to go out with. Give me a hug and a few hundred dollars before you leave!"

I covered my mouth in disgust and walked away, not caring what else was being said. I don't understand why Anita dealt with that type of shit, ain't nobody gonna be living up in my shit with no job, eating, shitting, sleeping, and fucking for free. Shit, Anita, my best friend and all, but homegirl got real issues!

They walked out the room hand in hand, and all I did was put a fake smile on my face and asked Anita if she was ready. Before we walked out the door, li'l Micheal ran out the room screaming, "Auntie Jay, I knew I heard your voice! Why didn't you come talk to me?"

Li'l Micheal was my little nigga. I love him like my own son and treat him as such. I bent down to kiss his cheek and said, "Because Auntie Jay is already late, so I couldn't come check on you, but I'll be picking you up tomorrow for the weekend, 'kay? So be ready."

"Okay, Auntie Jay, love you. Bye, Mommy, see you when you get home," li'l Micheal said before he went back in his room.

Chapter 3

In the car, I looked over at Anita and asked if she was okay because she looked troubled.

She said, "I'm fine, why do you ask?"

"I don't know, you look bothered, and don't lie and say that you're fine because I see your jaw twitching." When her jaw twitched, she was upset or thinking hard.

"Damn, I hate that you know me so well, but it's nothing I can't handle. Do you have all the materials this client request?"

"Yea, everything's in the trunk. I had to turn my phone off because Darnisha was blowing my shit up."

"What! What you do this time?"

"Shit, I ain't did shit, that's the problem. I been faithful. I haven't fucked Toya in a whole year since she found out I was still dealing with her on the low."

"Jay, you know I told you that shit will catch up with you sooner or later. I always tell you, you can't be a player and in a committed relationship. But knowing you, you will try it anyways." Anita was laughing while saying that.

"Yea! Yea! Whatever, but the point is I been good, but the way she naggin' me, it makes me wanna sneak and creep just to escape the headache and create a guilty conscience instead."

"You fucking stupid," she kept saying between laughs. "But I love you the same."

We pulled up to our destination, parked, and stayed in the car a second. I looked at Anita with seriousness written all over my face. "Nene, are you ready? Because this is a big client. We can't afford to make any mistakes with this one."

She looked at me with her game face on, and I knew then that she was ready, but before any meeting, I have to hear her say it.

"Yea, Jay, I'm ready! Let's get this done so we can celebrate after."

We both stepped out the car at the same time, went to the trunk to change clothes, and grabbed our materials. We put on our all-black custom-made Timbs, black Dickies, black pullover sweater, black beanie, black gloves, and black duffle bag. I pulled out the 12-gauge 187 magnum shotgun and put it in the empty duffle bag. By the time we were done seeing our client, the bag would be full of money, dope, and more guns.

Anita grabbed her twin Desert Eagles, screwed their silencers on, and put one in each hand. Looking at each other, we nodded and walked toward the vacant workshop. I'd been scoping this client for two weeks now. Every Thursday night at 7:00 p.m., he comes to count his money, bag his dope, and check on his ammunition. He always have two dudes with him that I plan to dust off with one bullet each.

It's now 7:15 p.m., and like clockwork, all three of them was sitting there at the table counting, bagging, and checking as I looked in the window. I signaled for Anita to see so she would know who and where to shoot. When it came to gunning a muthafucka down, Anita is that bitch. Now don't get me wrong, I'll kill a muthafucka in the blink of an eye, but Anita has a marksman eye just for that shit!

I crept in the shop unnoticed. They didn't even look up until I said, "All you bitch-ass niggas, stop what you doing and put your hands up!"

I had my gauge swinging and pointing at all three of them, but as usual, someone had to try to reach for their piece, and as soon as he did, his body dropped! The other two, looking stunned, immediately put their hands up. As I was walking toward them, I said, "Now this can run smooth or it can be messy, but I prefer smooth, what about y'all?"

As soon as the other one was about to say his answer, his body dropped. So only the client was stuck with his hands up. I shook my head, laughed, and said, "Damn, you, boys, are stupid. Who talks while getting robbed?" I was laughing again. "Listen, Mike, I want you to fill this bag up, and whatever doesn't fit, do you mind using yours?"

When he was about to answer, I quickly said, "Now don't answer, just do as you're told."

He walked around for a good seven minutes putting money, huns, and the ten bricks of dope he had in my duffle bag and his. That's when I heard him say under his breath, "I can't believe I'm getting hit by some bitch."

I stopped him and said, "I'm not just some bitch," and as I was about to say my next words, Anita came from the shadows and said, "We are those bitches, and we don't appreciate your disrespect, so make sure you tell the devil I said we'll see him later." Then his body dropped.

I grabbed the bags, looked at the three lifeless bodies around me, and put my gauge in my bag while making sure everything was okay. Anita checked each person's pulse to make sure that they were all what they appeared to be. Dead! While walking toward the door, we took one last look and left quietly. Back at the trunk, we changed back into our regular attire, put the clothes, guns, and duffle bag back into its proper place with an extra bag sitting next to it. I closed the trunk, walked around to the driver seat, and got in the car. Before I started the ignition, I turned and asked Anita, "Where to?"

She said, "Let's go to that karaoke joint inside of Cow Bowls over in Cerritos, I don't feel like big crowding it tonight."

I agreed, and we drove in silence, engrossed in our own thoughts as usual after we've seen a client. That's how it would be after every client for the last three years. We would ride away from the meeting in silence and not speak about it until we were in our office. My thoughts went back to our very first client. Anita and I were in a bar relaxing and talking among ourselves as usual when this brother walked in. He walked straight to the bar and looked at me. He then introduced himself as Tommy and that he had to hurry, to give him my number, and that he'll call me tonight. I laughed at him and told him that I don't mess around. What he did then was unbelievable. He turned to Anita and asked her for her number and told her she was cuter anyways.

Laughing, Anita said, "Nay! Tommy is it, how about you give me your number and I'll get at you?"

He gave her his number, not knowing that he was signing his death certificate. Hell, I didn't know we were initiating one. Once he left out of eyesight, I looked at Anita, and she said, "Jay, I hate when niggas think they all that and could get any bitch he wants. Hmph. Imma send his ass a big Bertha-looking bitch."

"Naw, Nene, I got a better plan, you call him, I watch him, and we'll go from there," I said.

"Girl, what you talking about?"

Then in a hush voice, I told her how I've always thought of doing some *Taxi Cab* type of shit, go in as men and get away as women. I told her how I've been planning for a long time and haven't found the right go-get-it person to hold it down with me. I also explained how no one would suspect us educated, successful women can be capable of robbing muthafuckas. How much money we'll make undercover and how we can go about it as a business in sales management who meets with clients?

Anita said, "Damn, bitch! You is crazy, but since I have skills as a marksman and you have skills in plotting and planning, then I guess we're in it to win it."

Ever since our first client, we've been getting better, our strategy was topflight. We turned out to be officially those bitches no one knew about or suspected when these big-timer bodies turned up missing.

Just as I was pulling up to our office, Anita said, "Jay, I'm tired, let's just drop this off and shoot me back to the crib."

"Okay. Nene, are you all right?"

"Yea. I'm fine, I just want to lay down and call it a night."

The office was a three-bedroom duplex in downtown Long Beach under Toya's baby cousin Tashanda's name. This house held all the materials, ammunition, and plans of our double life. No one had a key but me for the three years we've been using the house. I couldn't and wouldn't trust no one with a key. You had to be with me to enter the house and exit. It was a key to get in and a key to get out. The door was custom-made to my exact description. The house was barely finished with minimum furniture. The kitchen was set up like a minibar. I had all stocks and types of liquor in the cabinet. I had three rooms, but two were empty. The living room consisted of one dark brown suede couch, a wooden brown table in front of it, a stereo system, and a love seat that's an off-white.

In one room that has something in it, it just had two black dresser drawers with five compartments on each and a closet without change for our attire. The bathroom had the necessary toiletries and a few towels under the sinks in case of emergencies, and lastly, all the windows have black drapes in front of them so no nosy neighbor could look through. There were only four people who knew about this house and two that knew what was in the rooms.

As we got out the car, I went to the trunk, grabbed the bags and the key out the secret compartment in my trunk. I didn't ever carry these keys on my person. Safety precaution! Anita and I walked inside the house, she took off her heels and sat down. I poured her a drink, sat the bag down, poured one for myself, and stayed across from her. We didn't say anything for a while, loving the unwinding sound of peace.

Anita said, "How much you think we gonna get for those bricks?"

"I don't know, Imma put the word out that I'm letting them go for fifteen, but Imma wait at least a week or two before I put them out there."

"Right, as you should, so who and when is our next meeting?"

"Well, we have a meeting in about a week or two with a car that owns a jewelry store over on Manchester, but the dude got some undercover operations going on with them jewels. So Imma see exactly what's going on, then as usual, I'll call a meeting and give you the details."

"Okay, Jay, we don't really have too much to do tonight, so I'm ready when you are," she said, knocking the glass back and setting it down.

"Yeah, I'm ready, let's go."

Chapter 4

Before getting out the car, I kissed Jay's cheek and promised to call her in the morning before I got to the shop and after I drop li'l Micheal off. She then reminded me that he was spending the weekend with her and to have him ready by six o'clock.

When I walked in the door, Larnell was sitting his lazy ass in the same spot that I left him in. "Wassup, baby?" I said.

Larnell looked up with glazed eyes that was wide as saucers. "Nothing that you can't work with," he responded while looking at his dick. I caught on real quick.

"Let me go check on li'l Micheal and hop in the water then I'll be right with you, sweetie."

I walked to li'l Micheal's room to see him sleeping peacefully like all was well in his life. I went and sat on his bed, watching his chest rise and fall and looking at the innocence in his face. I love my baby even though he makes me miss his father. Micheal knew that he helped me create someone very special.

I kissed his cheek and whispered "I love you" in his ear then walked to my room.

In the room, Larnell was already naked in the bed, now watching our room's flat screen. I kicked off my heels and peeled out of my clothes. I strolled naked across the room, into the bathroom, and into the shower. I lathered up real quick because I was horny as fuck. I rinsed and stepped out well, walking back into the room.

I stood there for a second until Larnell looked up and said, "Damn, baby, bring yo sexy ass over here so I can beat your pussy up."

I willingly obliged. As I straddled his legs, I went in for a deep, long, passionate kiss, my juices immediately started flowing. He grabbed my ass cheeks, and I started humping the air in a grinding movement. Larnell flipped me over and started kissing my neck, trailing those kisses until he got to my titties. He then sucked on each one until they felt like little raisins. Larnell continued to go lower and lower with his kisses, then he reached my honey nest, and oh my, I couldn't catch my breath fast enough when he put his entire mouth over my pussy. I immediately came without a second thought. He sucked, licked, and pulled on that little man in the boat, and my lefts started shaking while I screamed in pure bliss.

"Larnell, baby, please," I moaned.

Grabbing his head up to mine, I kissed him, tasting my juices on his tongue, turning me onto something fierce. I turned him over and started sucking on his neck, down his throat, down his abs, then stopped at his midsection. His dick was so hard and split it looked like if I were to touch it, it would burst. I looked up at him to see him watching me with lust in his eyes. I licked my lips, slid down, and wrapped my mouth around his shaft.

As he humped my mouth, I was exploring his body with my hands the way he liked it while getting head. When I felt his thighs tightening, I removed my mouth and straddled him. When I felt his hardness inside me, I went to town squeezing and squeezing my muscles. Then I saw his eyes rolled behind his head, and I knew that he was about to cum. I rode faster and faster. I took us all the way until we both climaxed at the same time. I slid off of him, kissed him, and laid my head on his chest.

After catching his breath, Larnell said, "I'm sorry, Anita, for hitting you earlier."

Every time after sex is when we're at our best nowadays, and I already knew this was coming because Larnell was always on edge when he needed a hit. So this was nothing new.

"It's okay, baby, I understand. Let's just go to sleep because I don't want to be tired in the morning."

"Okay, baby, I love you."

"I love you too, Larnell."

*****

I jumped up when I heard the shower running. I already knew what was going on in the bathroom, but I got up, stretched, and walked in anyway. I grabbed my toothbrush, toothpaste, and stepped into the awaiting water. Seeing Larnell hit that pipe disgusted me no matter how many times I now saw him pulling on it. The smell was out of the ordinary, and it didn't sit well with my stomach. I hurried in the shower as fast as I can. While stepping out, Larnell handed me my towel, kissed my lips, and said, "Good morning, Anita! How did you sleep?"

I walked toward the dresser to pull out my underwear and bra. "I slept like the queen I am, my love, especially after that session last night."

Now walking to the bed to sit and lotion up, Larnell said, "Naw, baby, relax, let me do it."

This wasn't new, but it was a surprise because it's been awhile since he's been this nice.

"Larnell, we got the weekend to ourselves, starting at six tonight. So what you want to do?"

Looking up at me he said, "A lot of catching up on our quality time. I'll have plans by the time you come home from work."

I stood up, pulled out my Dereon jeans that made my ass look bigger, a black, fitted, simple shirt, some black heels, and silver accessories. I did my ponytail real quick, wrapped my robe around me, and walked out the room to go wake up my baby.

As I walked in li'l Micheal's room, he was already stirring, so I gently tapped him and said, "Sweetie, Auntie Jay would be here at six tonight, and it's only 6:50 in the morning, so we should get up, get dressed for school so the day can go by so you can see Auntie. Would you like that?" All I have to mention to get him up and moving was Auntie Jay.

He jolted up just as I thought and wrapped his arms around my neck and said, "Good morning, Mommy. What am I wearing today?"

"I don't know, honey, what do you want to wear?" He liked to get his own self dressed, so I asked him what he wanted.

"Aww, mommy, I'm in a rush today, can you pick out something?"

I laughed. "You are too much sometimes, and may I ask where are in a rush to?"

"Mom, I have to go to school first before I can go with Auntie Jay, so I'm in a rush to get to school."

Laughing and smiling adoringly at my son, I respond, "All right, Junior, go brush your teeth and wash your face while I set your clothes out and make you something to eat."

I walked to the closet when Junior ran out the room to the bathroom. I pulled out a pair of black Dickies pants, a button-up red-and-black plaid shirt, his favorite pair of white, red, and black Jordan's, then went to the drawer to get an undershirt. After I set his clothes at the foot of his bed, I went into the kitchen to scramble some eggs and fry a few pieces of bacon. I was putting the pot of hot water on for the grits when Larnell walked in the kitchen dressed. I turned and asked him where he was going.

He said, "Imma go with you to drop off Junior, then Imma drop you off at work and take the car to run a few errands, if that's okay with you?"

As I'm turning the bacon over and scrambling the eggs, I decided not to answer his question and asked one of my own. "Are you hungry? And how long will you need the car for?"

"Naw! I'm good on breakfast, but I don't know, I'll take you to lunch."

Li'l Micheal ran in dressed and flung his backpack on the couch and went to Larnell, saying, "Good morning, Dad."

"Wassup, little man. Why you all happy and chippery this morning?"

"Because Mom says that tonight I'm going with Auntie Jay for the weekend, so I need to speed the day up."

Larnell started laughing. "That's wassup, little man, so I take it you can't wait to get away from me and yo momma."

While Larnell was rubbing the top of his head, he said, "No, I love you both, but Auntie Jay is so much fun!"

I said, "Okay! Here, Junior, eat your food while I go get dressed. Larnell, come here!"

When I got to the room, I waited for Larnell to close the door. "L, where are you gonna be all day with my fucking car?"

"Anita, damn! I'm going to my folks' house then Imma take you to lunch, okay? Is that all right with you because I'm not trying to argue and I'm taking the car regardless."

I blew out a breath and threw my robe down. "Okay, you're right. I'm sorry, I don't want to argue. I'll be ready in a minute."

Larnell walked out the room, and I got dressed, mad at myself for not putting my foot down. Imma just buy the nigga a car, but fuck, Jay gon' be mad at me for tricking and denting my pockets once again. *Oh well,* I told myself, *money come, money go.* I walked in the living room dressed and ready with keys and purse in hand. Junior grabbed his backpack, and Larnell grabbed li'l Micheal's coat just in case he got cold later. We all walked out looking like a happy family.

It was quiet in the car besides Junior singing every song that came on. When I pulled up in front of his day care, I turned, unbuckled him, kissed his cheek, told him I loved him, and I'll see him at four. Then Larnell walked him inside. While Larnell was signing him in, I called Jay.

"Hello," she said with a groggy voice.

"Wake up, sleepyhead. I'm on my way to the shop, what time you coming in?"

A moan came through the phone. "I'll be there around ten, okay? I'll see you then."

I said all right and hung up. When Larnell got back in the car, I was already on the passenger's seat. I looked over at him. "Imma get you a car this weekend, so decide what you want, and we'll get it tomorrow."

He looked shocked but wanted to seem indifferent, so he just shrugged his shoulders. "All right, but why we can't share yours?"

I rolled my eyes and made sure my voice was leveled. "I need my car and you need a car, so we'll get you one, okay?"

He didn't respond, sensing my attitude I guess, so we rode to Jay's shop in silence. I'm the manager at the shop that Janikka owned. I wanted to be her partner, but she said that a beauty shop don't need a partner but she needed a manager. So every day, except Mondays when we're close, I'm opening up the shop at 8:30 a.m. and closing it at 8:30 p.m. As we pulled up to the shop, I saw all the beauticians and other workers standing around waiting for me with their cup of coffee or gossiping early in the morning. Jay's shop was in the heart of South Central, Los Angeles, on Main and Manchester.

Before I stepped out, Larnell said, "I'll see you around eleven thirty…twelve, Anita, so be ready."

I turned, looked at him, shook my head okay, and stepped out the car. I grabbed the keys out my purse and strutted to the front door, waving and saying good morning to those who spoke, thinking to myself *This is gonna be one long day* as I opened up the shop doors for business.

Chapter 5

When Nene called this morning, me and Darnisha were still asleep. Seeing that it's Friday and that Darnisha don't go in the office until nine thirty on Fridays, we always sleep in. The phone must've woken her up, too, because her ass was already on one. She's a morning freak, that's what I love so much about her. She slid under the blanket and opened my legs. She kissed the inside of my left thigh, the right, then bit down before she started trailing the kisses to my pearly gates of heaven. Once her warm mouth touched my little lady, I arched my back and scooted myself closer to her mouth.

While she was licking and sucking on my pussy, I closed my eyes and interlocked my fighters in her hair. I threw the blanket off us so I could see her face while I fucked her mouth to reach my climax. When my legs started to shake, she grabbed ahold of my clit and sucked on it hard, just the way I like it. I moaned loud just as my juices flowed into her mouth. I pulled her up, kissing her roughly. Now super in the mood, I turned her onto her back, lifted her legs, then opened them wide so our pussies could bump clits expertly. I humped our pussies while kissing her passionately, moaning faster and harder as we neared another peak.

She moaned in my ear, "Harder, baby! Faster, Jay!" Then she screamed out in ecstasy.

I slid my kisses down and started sucking on her titties, loving the perkiness and fullness of them every time I saw them. I continued my kisses, trailing my tongue until I reached her honeypot. I lifted her legs and had them bent at the knees with my forearms holding them in place, then I went to war. My mouth against her prized possession, I licked, sucked, and swallowed all she had to give. When her third orgasm came, she bucked so hard the neighbors heard our headboard. I gave her pussy one last kiss and released her legs out of submission. Out of breath and glowing hard, Darnisha curled up on the bed.

I slapped her ass, laughed, and walked in the bathroom to shower singing "Forever My lady" by K-Ci and JoJo in the shower. Darnisha stepped in and grabbed my towel. I said, "Good morning to you too, sweetheart."

She looked up with that so-what-you-got-me face.

"Yea, whatever," I laughed aloud because I couldn't hold it no longer. "Somebody needs another round, I think." I pushed her against the shower wall, and she hurriedly started talking.

"Nuh-uh! No, you don't. I gotta go to work, and you got to get to the shop." She kissed me then said, "Unless you want my daddy to put out an APB, then we need to shower and get out fast."

We kissed a little longer, washed each other's bodies, and got out. Back in the room, I said, "I'm going to go pick up li'l Micheal at six tonight for the weekend, so what should we do with him?"

"I don't know, we can take him to that Gameworks arcade on Saturday and the beach Sunday, and tonight we'll take him to go see Alvin and the Chipmunks Anniversary!"

"That's fine with me because you know, I really don't care what we do as long as my little nigga is here with me, I'm cool."

"I know, Jay. I love li'l daddy too, so what are you doing for lunch today?" she asked.

I sat there in thought for a minute before I answered her question. "Well, Imma be pretty busy at the shop catching up on paperwork, so I'm not taking lunch out, I might just eat a sandwich from the deli around the corner from the shop like I usually do."

Darnisha walked over, sat on my lap, and kissed my eyelids. "Okay, baby, but this weekend, me and li'l daddy have all your undivided attention, right?"

I kissed her lips, lightly pushed her up, and said, "Right, now come on let's get dressed before I think of other ideas."

I wanted to be simple today, so I grabbed my all black Juicy Couture sweat suit with a white tank top underneath and my all white shell toe Adidas. I grabbed my Tiffany lock chain with me and

Darnisha's picture inside and my matching bracelet. I put my cell phone and keys in my pocket, grabbed my credit card and $500 in cash out my drawer, and put it in my other pocket. I walked to the mirror, unwrapped my hair, and combed it down, impressed with how fast it's grown since I cut my ends.

Just as I was thinking it, Darnisha said, "Damn, baby, your hair is growing fast, and it looks so healthy."

"I know, babe, I was just thinking that same exact thing. Are you almost ready to get out of here?"

"Um, yeah. Let me just grab my handbag."

I turned around to see her looking gorgeous in a navy-blue pencil skirt suit, with a white blouse underneath with the exact same Tiffany lock chain, matching bracelet with a pair of diamond stud earrings. She had the sexiest legs with even sexier ankles adorned in some white pointy heels, rocking a dazzling Tiffany ankle bracelet I bought her for her birthday last year. I was just thinking to myself, *Damn! My woman is beautiful.*

She caught me staring and shook her manicured hands at me saying, "Please, don't look at me like that before you persuade me to take my clothes back off. Now come on, let's go."

She grabbed her keys off the dresser and headed for the door. I was right behind her. "Let's stop at Starbucks before we get on the freeway."

When I locked the house up, she said, "Naw, baby, you go ahead. I'm not trying to be late and hear Daddy mouth. I'll call you on my break."

I walked her to her Lexus, opened her car door for her, and kissed her. "Okay, baby…oh! And before you come home, stop and get some ice cream and snacks for your li'l daddy so it can already be in the house."

She nodded her head, rolled down her window, and yelled out while driving off. "Okay, love! See you later!"

I waved and watched her drive off down the block before I got in the Benz. I looked in the player to see what I heard in last. I took out the Keyshia Cole because I wasn't in that type of mood. Instead, I put in my *Double Up* CD by R. Kelly and hit the streets. I stopped off at Starbucks and went inside because the drive-through was full as the inside. While I was waiting for my order, a familiar voice whispered in my ear, "Wassup, sexy?"

I smiled despite myself and turned to see the yellowest thing with some long, black, wavy hair standing at 5'4" with her 32C cup staring right at me with her hazel eyes that I loved so much, and those lips all glossed up like that should be a crime. I snapped out of my undying lust and said, "Good morning to you too, Toya. What are you doing here so early, you're usually still asleep."

Toya smiled. "Damn, Jay, it's good to see you too, lover girl. So how are you doing?" she asked.

Not one to let my discomfort show, I hurried up and spoke trying to get it over with. "Look, Toya, wassup, what do you want? I don't have time for your game."

She smacked her lips. "So it's like that! Now that you're shacked up with a girl, you have to rush me off like I'm just some bitch you done fucked?"

I blew out an impatient breath. "Naw, Toy, it's not even like that. You know you'll always be my sweet cakes, but the Mrs. found out because someone didn't know how to wait for me to return her call instead of blowing my ship up like we was in Afghanistan."

Laughing, she put her hand on my cheek and rubbed my ear, knowing that's my spot. She leaned in and whispered in my ear, "Jay, it's been too long, and I promise I'll be good this time. Can I, please, have some of your time today?"

Not thinking clearly and knowing I miss her as much as she misses me, I said, "Come by the shop at 1:00 p.m., and we'll go get a room real quick to catch up on old times, okay?"

She stepped back, smiled, and said, "Okay, Jay, I'll be there at one. And, Jay, they been calling your name for your order."

I smiled back, shook my head, and walked to the counter. I grabbed my order, headed for the door, and turned to yell over my shoulder, but I saw her talking so I just walked out.

Back in the car and on my drive to the shop, I thought about Toya. We were together four years before she started talking about marriage and kids. Don't get me wrong, I want to get married and have a child, but I didn't want that with her. Toya is beautiful, but she's too hood. Born and raised in the Jordan Down projects on 103rd in Watts, her entire family is from Grape Street. I'm not into that. Our four years together was sweet and very sexual. Man, the sex was mind-blowing. Even after we broke up, I was still fucking her because in her mind somewhat, somehow, she thinks the pussy will get me to come back. I don't put that shit in her head, so I don't know where it comes from. Even after I met Darnisha and got into a relationship with her, I was still fucking Toya until her stupid ass kept calling my phone one night when I was with Darnisha. I remember that night, Darnisha was like, "Who the fuck keep calling you and why the fuck aren't you answering, Jay?"

All night, she kept on saying, "I know it some bitch, so just answer it."

I didn't answer it, but the next morning, I didn't know that Darnisha had followed me and saw me arguing with Toya. Then I hugged and kissed her, and Darnisha came out of nowhere yelling and screaming.

I'm like, "What the fuck are you doing here, Darnisha?" Basically, after all that commotion, I left Toya alone and kissed Darnisha's ass for two weeks. Me and Toya talked now and then, and I even seen her once in the club, but I haven't been dealing with her. But right now when I saw them lips, those titties, and then the eyes batting at me, I gave in to the urge of wanting to fuck her on sight. As I pulled up in front of my shop, I shook my thoughts off away from Toya. Parking and getting out, I sucked in the fresh air and watched all the hustling and bustling on the busy streets of South Central. I nodded my head to someone who waved and mentally prepared myself for the verbal lashing I was about to get from Anita when she sees Toya walk in the shop at one this afternoon.

Chapter 6

As I was walking toward the front door of the shop, I could hear all the chattering and gossiping from outside the door. I smiled to myself, knowing that opening JAY'S ALL-PURPOSE BEAUTY SHOP was the best thing I could've done for this community. You could come here and get your hair weaved, cut, trimmed, braided, washed, and dyed. You could get waxed, have your eyebrows waxed and arched. The men can come get cut and trimmed. And last but not least, you could come kick it and gossip with the neighborhood folks.

I haven't had an incident since I opened up for business three years ago. I have eight beauticians, two clerks, two shampoo girls, one masseuse who handles waxing and arching, and Anita as my manager. She's the best at what she does and so efficient with everything. She kept all the cashier receipts totaled to the exact amount. Anita didn't understand why she couldn't be my partner until I explained to her that owning a beauty shop only requires one boss and usually requires the boss to have a manager if I'm not gonna be there all day all the time and because I won't be able to manage the beauticians, clients, and other workers there on a daily basis.

Anita is in charge of collecting the booth fees every first of the month. All my beauticians' pay is $650, my barbers fee is $400, and my masseuse fee is $200. Anita is also in charge of paying the clerks and shampoo girls with a company check of $250 a week. This was the hood, these women can braid, gossip, sell dope, and cook at the same time, why not have them in my shop so my business can boom? I have five women beauticians and three male barbers that all get along fine.

I walked in to hear everyone stop their conversations to speak to me. I heard all types of "Hey, Jay!" "Damn, who that?" "Hi, boss lady!" "Shit! She fine."

I said, "Good morning, everyone! What's going on?" Then I heard a lot of "Shit, nothing" "Same ole same song."

I just laughed and continued toward the back when Tashanda stopped me in my tracks. She asked, "Jay, can I talk to you for a minute?"

Now Tashanda, she's real cool, that's Toya's baby cousin on her daddy's side, so she's not as hood but still ghetto as fuck. She reminded me of Kim Parker off that show *The Parkers* on BET. Only thing missing was the laugh. Tashanda is one of my clerks and always had her nails, hair, and feet done. She was one of those ghetto fabulous broads that will tell you in a minute that you are crazy for wasting all that money on the name brand expensive shit when you can rock the hell out of some Baby Phat, Rocawear, and Ecko Red with some heels.

"Wassup, Tashanda, everything okay?"

She lowered her voice, "Yea, but I just wanted to ask if I can have Tuesday off next week because I have to go visit Damonte in jail up at Wayside County Jail for the weekend until I can come up with the money for his bail."

I shook my head in sympathy. "Come back here in my office in five minutes so I can talk to you, all right?"

"Okay," she said and walked off.

I went and knocked on Anita's door, we have our own offices. The way the building was reconstructed, I had it made down to my exact design. When you walk in the shop door, you had waiting chairs and two lounge couches.

You had the clientele check-in and appointment-making desk, then right behind the desk, you had four chairs lined up on each wall that had leather seats the color of lavender and white, with a walkway down the middle. When you continue to walk the aisle, there's the sinks and dryers. Then we had a room for waxing, massaging, and eyebrow plucking on the left.

Across from there, you had a customer's little bathroom with a toilet and sink, no mirror because there's mirrors in front of each booth so the clients can watch themselves get done up by my girls. Then you had the worker's little locker room where they store their purses, lunch, or whatever they have with their personal key. Right next to the locker room, you had me and Anita's office. They're just little rooms with a desk and chairs, but the only difference between mine's and Anita's was she had a file cabinet with all my important documents. Such as leasing papers, mortgage bill, utility bill, tax bill, bank statements, check stubs, and the worker's files and portfolios that she maintained.

I waited a second more then pushed the door open to see Anita staring at the picture of her, li'l Micheal, and Larnell on her desk.

I sat down in one of her comfortable twin chairs and asked her what's on her mind. She took a second to answer, then she looked up at me. "Jay, I think I'm pregnant."

I was shocked and stunned. I asked the stupidest question. "How? I mean, I know how, but did you miss a period or something? How do you know, did you take a test?"

I was talking so fast, shaking my head, and throwing her question after question, not wanting to believe my best friend is pregnant again by a nothing-ass nigga. The first time that she found out she was pregnant by Larnell, she didn't tell him. She told me, and I immediately told her to get rid of it. Larnell is a scumbag to me, and I knew she loves him, but I was really hoping she would drop him after a few months of dating. Shit, was I wrong. The nigga moved in with her after a few months and hadn't left since. Now she's pregnant supposedly again, and we promised each other the next time that she would tell him because she felt so bad afterward.

I continued shaking my head when I saw tears coming out her eyes. I knew then that whatever was going on with Anita wasn't just about her so called "pregnancy."

Looking up at me, she said, "Jay, I don't know. I have an appointment scheduled for Monday to confirm my thoughts and feelings. I just need you to go with me at 10:00 a.m."

I looked at my watch. "Okay, Nene, I'll go. I was just stopping by to let you know I was here, but I'll be back in a little bit so we can talk because right now, I have to speak with Tashanda about something."

"Okay. Is everything all right with her?"

"Yeah, just a personal issue she going through with Damonte."

I got up to walk out when she said, "Janikka, make sure you come back."

I nodded my head okay and walked into my office. Now, my office had amateur painting on the wall because I love supporting up-and-coming talent. Two of the same exact twin chairs from Anita's office faced the front of my wood-grained desk. It had a swivel chair behind it. I had pictures of li'l Micheal, me, and Darnisha and me and Anita everywhere in the office. I had the prettiest sculpted model of two women joined together on my desk that symbolizes the joint of two women can be a beautiful thing. As I was sitting there with thoughts of Anita's situation in my head, there was a knock on the door. Already knowing who it was, I told her to come in and close the door behind her. I ushered her to sit down and get comfortable. I leaned back in my chair and asked Tashanda what Damonte was in jail for.

Tashanda had been with Damonte for four years now. They were about two and a half years in when me and Toya split, so it's been a while since I've seen Monte, but he's a cool car. He's a known hustler around these parts and has had minor problems with the law, so I wanted to know how serious his charges were.

She said, "They busted him with four packs of bagged-up quarter pieces of crack. So they're charging him with possession and intent to sell."

I nodded my head in understanding then asked her what the bail was.

"Fifty thousand dollars. But through bails bond, they want 5,000, and I only have 3,500 right now. Jay, this shit is bullshit! I don't want my man sitting in no damn county jail!" Her eyes started tearing up, so I handed her a tissue.

"Believe it or not, I know what you're going through. Tashanda, I don't know if you know, but my older brother is up at Ironwood State Prison doing thirteen years flat, and he only been down half of that. So I worry about him all the time, and, of course, he's okay financially because I take care of him. Shit, I even go see him every month once, but it's still fucked up being in that type of situation. So what Imma do is Imma give you that $1,500 you need to bail him out, and you, guys, get it back to me when y'all can so that way you don't have to go up there to only see him but pick his ass up!"

I started laughing, and Tashanda looked at me with a fresh pair of tears then hopped out her seat and ran to come hug me. "Thank you, Jay! I swear we'll get the money back to you."

"Don't worry about it, you're like family. When you see me come back from lunch, come back to my office and I'll give it to you then, all right?"

She said all right then got up to leave.

I sat there a minute in silence until my desk phone started ring. I answered, "Jay's all-purpose hop hot, may I help you?"

Then Darnisha voice came through the phone. "Hey, baby, what you doing?"

"Aww nothing, just thinking about you, my love. What about you?" I could see her smiling all the way through the phone.

"Nothing, just taking a little break and wanted to hear your voice."

"Oh, is that right? Well, since you put it like that, I miss you too."

"Yeah, right, anyways, babe, Daddy asked if we can make it to Malibu on Saturday for a barbeque. What you think?"

I stayed there thinking a minute because Richard's house was nice with a backyard that had a swimming pool, and not to mention his barbeque steaks are off the chain.

"Yeah, that's cool, just let him know we have li'l Micheal with us and ask him what he wants us to bring."

"Okay, baby. I'll ask and let him know, but I'm going to get back to work. I'll see you at home."

"All right, I love you, Nisha!"

"Love you too…bye!"

After I hung up the phone, I checked my watch to see that it was already twelve o'clock. So I walked to Anita's office to find a note saying, "Out to lunch with Larnell, be back in a little bit."

I crumpled the note, wondering why she just didn't come tell me but remembered that my door was closed while speaking with Tashanda. I walked out the back and to the front of the shop to hear and see business booming as usual.

I waved at my girl, April, a regular client in my shop, and on occasion, I'll go party with her, but she's a ghetto and a cold drunk. I went to go to chat with her for a minute. As soon as I was within earshot, April said, "Jay, girl, you rocking that sweat suit. What is that, Juicy Couture?"

"Yeah, girl, what's been up with you? I haven't seen you in a while."

"Girl, I was in here last week, you know. Tony hooks my shit up every Friday. Where you been?" she asked.

"Around, but Imma catch you in a minute, okay?" I walked off quick, not liking people in my business. I went around talking to clients and approving of some of my worker's skills.

As I was talking to Shay, one of the shampoo girls, Toya walked in strutting and looking every inch of the beauty she was putting you in mind of Christina Milian in *Love Don't Cost a Thing*. Heads turned as she stopped at the desk, then she looked up to see me. While she was walking toward me, the sway of her hips screamed for attention. I saw eyes bucking and mouths open. I knew why. Shit, Toya had one of the most perfected round handful asses I've ever seen inside and outside of the clothes.

She had a slim waist, flat stomach, and hips that curved to form her perfect ass with some nice C-cup titties. Toya knew she was a sexy light-skinned female, but the ghetto and goodness in her always showed in most of the shit she do. Like right now, she had on a Baby Phat jean skirt suit, a light pink Baby Phat shirt underneath with some silver open toe Jimmy Choo heels, a diamond tennis brace-let that matched her ankle bracelet, some little silver hoop earrings looking beautiful as ever but chewing on a piece of bubble gum and popping it loud every few chews, knowing I hate that shit. When she reached me, I looked at her mouth to see her lips glossed, but she knew I wasn't looking at that. She pulled the gum out her mouth, and after I nodded, she asked if I was ready.

"Yeah, let me go close up my office door."

As I was walking away, I heard Tashanda greeted her cousin and could only imagine the facial expression she had. On our way out, I told Tony to hold down the shop until me or Anita get back.

Tony nodded "Okay," and I grabbed Toya's hand and headed out the door.

Chapter 7

Once in the parking lot, we hopped in Toya's car and drove off. In the car, I started talking, "Toya, who you fucking with because I don't need no problems and I don't want no bitch running up in my shop or scratching up my car writing 'Stay away from my woman' on my windows."

We both started laughing. "Jay, shut up! I'm not with nobody, but I am fucking on some bitch named Diamond that work at the strip club over on Western and Rosecrans. And before you say anything, she's very clean and don't fuck around like them other hoes."

I asked, "How do you know that, Toya? We going to your house! But like I was saying, how do you know that and how long have you been dealing with this 'Diamond bitch' as you say?"

"Because I watched her before I approached her, and we went to go get tested together."

I left the situation alone because we were pulling up in Toya's two-bedroom apartment parking garage. She only lived a few blocks away from my shop. I have visited her place numerous times, but something seemed different as I walked inside. I couldn't quite pinpoint it because she still had all black suede couches, her favorite lavender recliner chair, with the glass table in front of a thirty-six-inch screen TV hooked up to the speakers. Her dining room set was the same four-seater square glass table with the black suede seats surrounding it and that vase of white and red roses sitting on top that she changed every week.

As I walked farther down the hall, still trying to figure out what's missing, I peeped in the bathroom to see that the black and charcoal gray setting was still the same. Then when I reached her room to see the black nightstands next to her queen-sized bed that had a new lavender comforter instead of gray, with new black-and-white throw pillows instead of lavender, I noticed what was missing. And not noticing, I said my thoughts out loud. I heard Toya say, "Jay, what did you expect? Of course, I took all the pictures down when I realized you weren't coming back to me a year ago."

I didn't know exactly what to say, so I walked over to her and kissed the lips I missed so much. After I disconnected our lips, I started taking her clothes off piece by piece. First the jacket, then the pink top. When I unhooked the bra, I grabbed ahold of titties as I sucked on each nipple, giving them both a fair share of my spit. I was unhooking her skirt, so when the skirt fell, she kicked it from around her ankles. While continuing to go from nipple to nipple with my mouth, I put my hand down her underwear to feel that she was already hot and wet for me. I inserted a finger, and a moan escaped her mouth. I lifted up to kiss her once again then gently pushed her on her back onto the bed. I stepped back and pulled off my clothes.

I then lay in between her legs, kissing her again, loving the way the inside of her mouth was tasting. I slid her panties down while I was trailing my tongue down her flat stomach, stopping just to twirl on her belly piercing with my tongue, knowing that's her spot. As expected, she arched her back while I inserted my fingers in her once again. I then moved my way to her clit and started flicking my tongue back and forth and finger fucking her at the same time. I replaced my fingers with my mouth, wanting to taste the sweetness of her pussy. She opened her legs wider and continued to grind her hips on my tongue.

"Ohhhh, Jay, this pussy misses you so much."

In between my licks and slurps, I said, "And Jay misses this pussy too." It seemed right when I said that she started cumming hard.

I sucked all the juices up then lifted up to kiss her. She flipped me over and started kissing me hard then went straight down between my legs to find me dripping wet and anticipating the warmth of her mouth to find its place. Once her mouth touched my spot, I let out a soft-sounding moan. She made a V shape with her fingers, placed them on my pussy lips, and went all the way there with my pearl tongue. I had one hand on my titty and the other on her hand, grabbing a hold of her hair and moving wildly under her mouth. I came long and hard. Panting, I told her "Get on the bed and scoot up" while reaching for the bottom drawer on the nightstand to grab my strap-on dildo, hoping it was still where I expected it to be. When I felt it, I stood up, stepped through the jockstraps, and adjusted the belt.

I got back on the bed, wanted to fuck Toya from behind. I told her to flip over and bend at the knees. When she did, I kissed each ass cheek, rubbed her clit with my hand to make sure she was ready for me, then I penetrated her with the eight-inch cock. Loving the way I saw her pussy fitting around my cock, I slapped her ass and grabbed ahold of her hips and settled into a rhythm. I started to feel my own juices flowing while I was fucking her. I started speeding it up when I saw her grinding back. I grabbed her hair and pulled her head back and fucked her hard while rubbing on her clit. Feeling her climax coming, I concentrated on hitting her spot.

She started telling out, "Oh yes! Yes! I'm cumming, Jay! Right there! Right there!"

While she was moaning, panting, and twisting wildly underneath my hold, I thrust hard inside of her for the last time and saw all the juices flowed down my cock and between her thighs while feeling my own juices coming down my thighs. I collapsed on her back and kissed her neck.

A minute or two later, I looked at my watch to see it was almost three o'clock. I lifted up off the bed, loosened the belt, and pulled off the cock then walked in the bathroom in her room. I set the strap-on in the sink and let the warm water run on it while I soaped up a washcloth to wipe in between my legs. I wouldn't get in the shower because that's a dead giveaway for me to go home smelling all fresh and out the shower. When I walked back in the room to put on my clothes, Toya was straightening out the comforters and throw pillows naked.

I was looking at her ass then said, "Toy, you better get ready to go before I end up doing something to get us both in trouble."

She looked up smiling and started walking toward the bathroom. "Um, remember you're the one with the woman, not me!" she said laughing.

"Yeah, whatever, Toya. I'm not the one that got to remember that. You do," I said and walked out the room, knowing that was a low blow.

After admiring Toya's artwork on her living room walls for a minute, she walked out in some Rocawear jeans and a white Rocawear T-shirt. I turned and asked, "Why did you change?"

"Because I have to make a few stops after I drop you off at the shop."

I didn't respond to that, and we walked out the house.

After she locked up and we were back in the car, that was when she spoke again, saying, "When will I be able to see you again?"

Bobbing my head to the music she was playing, I replied, "I don't know, Toya, let me see wassup then I'll call you, all right?"

I could tell that she was about to get a little attitude, so I quickly said, "Maybe next week, but I can't make no promises because I have a lot of shit to do these next few days." Seeming to put her at ease a little bit, I continued, "I have an appointment on Monday and a meeting on Tuesday, so I might be able to see you on Wednesday or Thursday."

"Okay, Jay, just don't keep me waiting. I already told you I'm kind of seeing somebody, so I know we're just fucking with no strings attached."

Feeling relieved that she already know wassup, I said "All right, cool" and was about to get out of the car when she said, "No matter who I'm with, Janikka, I will always love and want you."

I looked back at her and said "I know" then stepped out the car. When I closed the door, I turned to wave so she could drive off, all the while thinking to myself, *I done fucked up!*

Chapter 8

When Larnell called my phone to tell me that he was outside, Jay was still in the office with Tashanda, so I left her a note telling her I was leaving. When I walked out the shop, Larnell was parked in front of the shop standing outside the passenger door with it open. When I reached him, he grabbed me by my waist and pulled me into his arms. I hugged him back with my arms wrapped around his neck, kissing his lips. Every time I'm in his arm, I remember how much I love him. I leaned back, looking into his eyes, and smiled. As I got in the car, he closed the door, ran to his side, jumped in with a smile on his face.

He said, "Baby, why you smiling so hard?" He looked at me with that smile still on his face. "Anita, baby, I got a surprise for you, and before you say anything, this weekend I wanna make up for all our lost time we haven't spent loving each other."

I just stayed back, wondering what type of surprise he has for me because I wasn't really listening to what he was saying. Larnell gets nice when he wants something or when he's about to disappear for a few days. I recently found out that during the time of his supposed to be business trips he was holed up in somebody's hotel room fucking a bitch and sucking on the glass dick. I knew I'm stupid to still be with his sorry crackhead ass, but I love my man; besides his drug habit, he's the sweetest, most loving man I ever met. He treats li'l Micheal like his own son and been the father figure that li'l Micheal lacked. Ever since I pressed charges on Micheal and testified against him in court, I haven't been looking over my shoulder, wondering when he was gonna come sneak up on me.

I couldn't raise my son in that type of home, but now it's happening all over again, but no so much like before. I guess I was lost in thought the entire ride because I barely noticed when we pulled up to the park. Larnell turned off the engine, reached for my hand, kissed it, then got out. He opened the trunk, grabbed a basket and blanket. I got out the car looking at him then the basket and thinking to myself, *No, he didn't...*

As was tuning into my thoughts, Larnell said, "Come on, baby, we haven't done this in a while."

Grabbing my hand, we walked up the park, already knowing our destination. When we reached the top of the hill, Larnell laid the blanket out and set down the basket.

"Sit down, baby, and relax!"

I sat down, smiling and remembering how we used to come to Jesse Owens Park all the time, in this same exact spot on the hill talking, Larnell holding me in his arms while we planned our future together. Larnell reached in the picnic basket and pulled out two champagne glasses, some red wine, fruit salad, ham and cheese sandwiches, sour cream and onion chips, and a little bowl of garlic dip. All I could do was smile, reach over, and kiss him on the lips.

He pulled back and looked at me with those tantalizing eyes and said, "I love you, Anita."

He grabbed the champagne bottle, popped the top off, and poured some in our glasses. He grabbed them both, handed on to me, and said, "To our long-needed weekend."

We toasted, ate, and talked about good times. It felt good to sit there and spend some alone time with my man, reminiscing and planning our weekend together. I looked down at my watch and wondered how the time went by so fast. It was already two o'clock. I looked up at Larnell and said, "Baby, I'm enjoying myself so much with you right now, but I have to get back to the shop."

"It's okay, babe. Imma pick up li'l man at four, take him to McDonald's, then swing by the shop and wait for you to close up, how does that sound?"

"That's fine, but you two don't have to come to the shop until about five fifteen."

"All right, but come on, let's get going before Jay starts trippin' on you being gone so long."

I didn't respond because I knew he was being funny. Instead I grabbed and folded the blanket after he picked up the empty containers, bottle, then rolled up the chips. I had a slight buzz from the wine, but I wasn't on the verge of drunk. I rode back to the shop holding Larnell's hand whenever he didn't have them both on the wheel. Me being pregnant was the last thing on my mind then. I just wanted to dwell on the good time that I was having with Larnell and wishing it would never end. When we pulled up in front of the shop, I kissed Larnell and told him that I'll see him at five.

I walked in the door of the shop on autopilot, buzzed, and happy. I was waving to somebody when Tony said, "Why you smiling so big, Anita? Did that nigga Larnell propose or something?" He laughed.

"No, my man just makes me so happy." I made a little face to her then asked, "Is Jay still here?"

"Naw, Jay left around one a little after you with Toya but said she'll be back."

My mouth dropped open. All I said was "Okay" and started walking toward the back thinking to myself, *Ain't that 'bout a bitch, she back fucking with that hoe.* I can't stand Toya's ghetto ass, I've always hated her for Jay. I was so happy when Janikka met Darnisha and started falling for her. Hell, I encouraged Jay to continue seeing Nisha even though I was depressed going through my personal issues. I loved to see Jay happy. That bitch Toya is a sneak. I wonder if Janikka knew that she's fucking with that stripper over at the Paradise Palace. If she didn't know, I'll be sure to inform her when she comes back.

Thinking about her being with Toya blew my buzz off. Right when I was about to call her, she walked into the shop smiling, looking like me a minute ago. I was walking toward her when she looked up and saw the expression on my face, knowing I had something to say about her lunch break. She met me halfway then said, "'Sup, Nene, you back from lunch. How'd it go?"

I smiled, wrapping my arm in hers, walking us both toward the back where we can talk in private. Sometimes the way we were made people think that we were fucking each other. Now don't get me wrong, my girl is fly. Shit, I looked at her as a black version of Beth Porter on that hot series *The L Word* on Showtime.

Janikka is beautiful with some 36C-cup titties, slim waist, flat stomach, weighing about 150 pounds, with shoulder-length black hair, and standing at 5'5", she was a package. Smart, she always dressed to kill, looking sophisticated in her suits. My girl was all woman who loved women. I'm all woman who loved some dick, big black dick at that. I'm just concerned with the money-hungry hoes she attracted, that's why I can't stand Toya, the bitch was a gold digger who portrayed not to be.

When we stepped in the office, I rolled my eyes and said, "Well, my lunch was fine, but I wondered what you ate for lunch, considering who you left the shop with."

I could tell that Jay was aggravated by what I said, but I was feeling good and didn't give a fuck.

She snapped back, "What I ate for lunch is none of yo damn business. And since when did you start questioning me about who and what I'm eating?"

"Well, I'm not the one that was just sayin' 'Oh, I'm not fucking with Toya, I'm faithful…it's been a year.'"

She rolled her eyes and let out a sigh. "Look, Nene, I got what I'm doing, okay? You need to worry about you being pregnant again by that broke-ass nigga you got living in your house, eating and fucking for free!"

Looking at her face, I could tell that she wanted to take it back as soon as she said it, but it was too late. The damage was done.

"Get out, Jay!" I screamed.

"Nene, I'm sorry…I didn't—"

I cut her off. "Get out, Jay. I don't wanna hear it. I'll have my li'l man ready by six o'clock when you come get him. You've said all you need to say to me today."

When she walked out, I sat down trying to keep the tears from coming down my face. Jay was right about Larnell, but I loved him to death. She wouldn't understand that because she's selfish. All she worried about was herself. Jay always thought that she was better than me at everything. Sometimes she'll make me feel like I needed her to survive and maintain. I hated Janikka at times because of that. Right now was one of those times I couls kill her for talking that shit to me. Jay never liked Larnell ever since we've been together, and I don't know why, but it seems it got worse when I told her he lost his job. Of course, I didn't tell her about his drug habit and the fact that he never had a job, that would've been the end of a lot of things for me.

I was giving myself a headache sitting there in the office. So I called Larnell and told him to come pick me up. As I walked out my office and to the front door of the shop, I didn't bother to let Jay know that I was leaving, but I couldn't help to think that if I ever had to choose between Jay and Larnell, it wouldn't be a good look.

Chapter 9

Back in my office I was cursing myself out because I should've held my tongue, but Anita was getting on my damn nerves yelling and asking me about Toya like she was my woman or something. I mean damn! Oh well, she'll get over it. When I go to pick up li'l Micheal tonight, I'll apologize and leave it at that. But right now, I had more important shit on my mind instead of worrying about her and her broke-ass crackhead ass nigga. Anita thought that I didn't know Larnell smoked that shit, that's why I despise his ass, and for Anita not to tell me just makes me not trust her even more. It was a time when Anita told me everything with no exceptions.

I pushed that aside and dialed the number I was looking for, then a voice said, "Hey, you."

"Wassup, Cook, how's it going?"

"Well, you know it's going as usual. Travis sends his love and can't wait to see you this Sunday."

"Well, you know it's going as usual, but can I drop by tonight around 8:30?"

"Yeah, that's fine I'll see you then."

"Okay, peace!"

When I hung up the phone, I couldn't help smiling. If I had to do time in prison, I'd want to have it like my older brother Travis had it. Cook was a correctional officer at Ironwood State Prison in Blythe, California. I met up with her once a month and gave her fifty-two grams of heroin, one ounce of crystal, and two ounces of kush for him personally. Cook and my brother had been together going on for three years. Cook had been down and loyal to my brother ever since he cracked her, and I knew the extra money she's making was a plus. My brother doing thirteen years for a bank robbery that went sour coincidentally after he'd been doing bank licks since he was sixteen years old. Travis had been down goin' on six years now, and I made it my business to see him once a month and twice the month of his birthday in December.

I love my older brother and will do whatever he asked of me while he's doing his state bid. Deep in thought, there was a knock on the door. I yelled for them to come in. I looked up to see Tashanda coming in. *Just in time,* I thought. Reaching in the bottom-left drawer of my desk, I pulled out the shop emergency cashbox. I grabbed a rubber band roll then undid another and pulled five hundred dollars off that then sat the money on the desk. While I closed the lid and put it back in the drawer, Tashanda grabbed the money saying "Thank you" but still not moving toward the door. I asked her wassup.

She said smiling, "I'm not tryna be nosy, but you and Toya back seeing each other?"

For some reason, I knew she was about to ask me something about Toya, and she was anticipating and eager to hear my response, so instead I just brushed it off.

"If that's what you think, then that's what you think, but I got a few calls to make, so I'll holla at you later."

She smiled and walked out the door. Sitting my office alone once again, I picked up the phone and placed another important call because I knew that she was about to chew me out after hearing that voice message she left on my phone.

Darnisha picked up on the first ring yelling, "Where the fuck you been, Janikka, and don't think about lying because I called the shop and they said you left!" Before I could get a word out, she continued yelling. "I thought you said you wasn't going out to lunch today, or was it you just didn't want to go with me?"

When I was finally able to get a word in, I yelled, agitated, "If you must know, I went down to the deli then went window shopping at that jewelry store on Manchester before I headed back to the shop. And, Darnisha, I'm not about to be dealing with stupid shit every time you can't reach me on my goddamn cell phone!"

Then I hung up the phone without even giving her a chance to respond. Not feeling guilty at all about lying to her just now because she's been getting on my last fucking nerves these past few months. As soon as I leaned back in my chair, my cell phone rang. I looked at the screen, saying it better not be Darnisha's silly ass, and seeing the familiar number on the screen made me smile. I picked it up and waited for the usual recording to finish.

"You have a collect call from 'It's me.' To accept this call, press 5 now, to—your call is being connected."

"Hello?"

"Wassup, li'l sis, where the bitches at?"

"Very funny, my man, you know I'm committed, never faithful, but a fool in love. So how's it going, B.I.G.?"

"It's going, but I need to holla at you on some real serious business."

I immediately became alert because Travis never sounded this serious. Whatever was going on, I knew we couldn't discuss it on the phone, and while I was thinking it, Travis said, "Baby girl, you know we can't discuss it now, go along with your situation for tonight and make sure you're here Sunday."

"I will, B.I.G., I promise, but are you sure you're gonna be all right? Do you want me to come tomorrow?" then the recording said, "You have 120 seconds left."

"Naw, baby girl, I'll see you Sunday."

Then we talked some more about nothing and then he said, "I love you and remember what we live by. Trust no one and suspect all!"

"I love you too, and I'll never—" then the phone disconnected the call.

I hung up the phone, leaned back to ponder what could possibly be going wrong up there with my brother.

Ever since I was a little girl, Travis only called me "baby girl" when we were upset but trying to keep his anger under wraps because he didn't wanna scare me or make me worry. So I knew something was up, and for him to repeat our code to me had me all the way on edge. I thought I'd ask Cook that night how my brother was really doing. I looked down at my watch and saw that it was closing time, so I got up, straightened out the papers on this new business I was thinking about opening on my desk before walking out.

As I was locking up my office, I noticed that Anita's was already closed and could tell she was already gone. I heard all the workers in their locker room clowning and laughing as usual. I walked toward the front so I could double-check and make sure everything was cleaned up and looking in order.

While everybody was coming out the back room, Tashanda looked at me, smiled, and waved on her way out, followed by the rest. When Tony was walking out, I stopped her and asked her when Anita left, and she said that she left a couple of hours ago. I nodded, closed up the shop, then walked to my car. Anita always ran out when she was feeling some type of way after an argument, so this was expected. I called Anita's cell phone and didn't get no answer. Then I tried the house phone, and it ran a few times before a baritone voice said, "Hello."

I rolled my eyes because I swore I couldn't stand this bastard. "Where Nene at?"

Larnell's stupid ass always have something smart to say just like a bitch. "Now that's not how you ask to speak to someone when you call their home."

I was not in the mood to go back and fight with Larnell like I would usually, that's why I never called her house phone. He's a dumb fuck. I just told him that I was on my way and to tell Anita to have my li'l man ready when I got there then hung up the phone.

While I was driving, my thoughts went back to Travis and the concern in his voice. I wondered what was going on with my B.I.G., then my thoughts went to Rick and his jewelry store. Rick had jeweler design pieces like Ann Taylor, Robert Tornell, Tom Binn, Eddie Borgo, Susan Foster, and Prada pieces out of this world. Rick told me that I could meet with him in a week and he'll show me plenty of pieces outside of the shop that aren't put on display and are cash only. Since the meeting was set up, I was trying to figure out exactly how Imma prepare myself for this particular meeting.

I put my thoughts aside while I was pulling up in Anita's driveway. I inhaled a deep breath to prepare myself upon entering that house with Larnell. That man just rub me the wrong way and always look like he's up to something sneaky!

Shaking my head, I got out of the car, walked up to the porch, then knocked on the door. I could hear li'l Micheal happily running toward the door, screaming "Auntie Jay! Auntie Jay!" with pure excitement in his voice. Larnell then pulled the door open and asked if I wanted to come inside, and I quickly said no and explained that I was in a rush. I saw Anita coming down the hallway with li'l Micheal's bag, and when she handed it to me, I asked her to step outside for a minute. I yelled to li'l Micheal and told him to wait in the car while I talked to his mommy real quick. He ran back to give Anita a hug and kiss then went to get in the car.

Anita closed the front door then crossed her arms over her chest, the way she does when she's irritated or doesn't want to be bothered about something. So I took that as my cue to speak first. "Nene, I apologize for the things I said earlier. They were rude and uncalled for."

She looked at me, and that was when I noticed the glazed over eyes. Not the kind of glazed over the eyes when you're smoking weed but the kind of eyes that pop out like saucers. I just stared in shock with hopes that my dawg, my best friend wasn't into smoking that shit!

"I'm cool, Jay, so don't trip. I'm really kinda in the middle of something, so I need to get back inside. Y'all have fun and call me when you on your way on Sunday to bring my baby back."

She swiped her hand across her nose then hurried and dropped them to her side as if she just noticed what she did.

"Are you all right Anita? You sick?"

"Naw, Janikka, damn. I just said I'm cool…shit!" then she walked in the house.

I stood there looking shocked because she knew I knew she was getting high off that shit. And decided not to make a scene in front of li'l Micheal, I just walked to my car, got in, and goofed off with my li'l man all the way to Cook's house. After I stopped by and hit her off with the goods, I called Darnisha on my way to the house to make sure she picked up the goodies for li'l man, told her that I'm not really feeling the theater tonight, and that I'm grabbing some pizza and a movie so we can stay in. She said cool and that was fine with her.

After I picked up the pizza and was on the way home, li'l Micheal said, "Auntie Jay, can I tell you something?"

I turned the music down then told him to continue.

"Every time I come home from school and when Mommy's gone, it smells funny in the house. I don't know what it is, but when I asked my daddy what that smell was, he said don't worry about it because it's grown folk business then sends me to my room."

"Li'l man, did you tell your mom what you're telling me?"

"Yes, ma'am. I told Mommy last night, and she said I wouldn't have to worry about that funny smell again, but today I smelled it before you came when Mommy told me to stay in my room."

"Aww, li'l man, I'm sure it's nothing, but I'll ask your momma what's going on, okay?"

"Okay."

We pulled up to the driveway, and li'l Micheal ran in the house before I could get the bags and pizza out the car. Li'l Micheal loved Darnisha as much as she loved him. We settled in and ate, then we watched *Cars 2* and *Puss in Boots* before Micheal fell asleep on the couch, which he usually does, and I couldn't understand why because he had his own guest bedroom upstairs next to mine.

After a while of sitting there with li'l Micheal in my arms, I carried him up to his room in the blanket and tucked him in. I got in the shower and went to bed, knowing that Darnisha felt some type of way because I didn't respond to her touching me.

Chapter 10

"Fuck, Larnell, stop yelling at me!"

"Bitch, don't tell me to stop yelling at yo punk ass. You did all that dope before I could even come back from making a run for your stupid ass!"

Swiping my nose from the burning sensation, I just leaned my head back before this nigga could blow my high. Thinking to myself, *When did it get this bad?* I was going through eight balls of coke every two days by myself without Larnell's help. And when Larnell didn't have crack, he would want to snort my shit. I was tired of his shit, he was never satisfied.

I just bought his ass a brand-new Cadillac Escalade in cash. Fresh off the lot, and all I'd been getting ever since was a headache. My baby will be home later on tonight, and I just tried to relax my body until then.

Li'l Micheal's been asking me about a funny smell that we walked into when I'm not home. All I could tell him was, "Don't worry about it because it won't happen again." When I told Larnell about smoking that shit in the living room while I'm gone, he slapped the snot out my nose and said, "This is my damn house, and I'll do as I please!"

I felt arms yanking me up, and I threw my eyes open to see this nigga Larnell grilling me down and babbling something. I just nodded because I really couldn't understand a word he was saying. Larnell pushed me back down on the couch then said, "You're a sorry bitch, and that's why you'll always be second rate compared to Janikka!"

I sat up and screamed at him, "FUCK YOU, NIGGA! And don't worry, that bitch won't be so perfect when I'm done with her ass!"

Larnell just looked at me with pity, grabbed my purse, took some money out, then walked out the house. I got up, kicked the door and grabbed my plate of candy, and sat down and fed my nose, thinking to myself how much I'm gonna love to see Janikka go down.

*****

Walking through the visiting room, my brother looked the same. Tall, light-skinned, short cut fade with a taper and muscles sticking out from under his khaki top button up and white tee under. He smiled when he saw me then made his way to our favorite table in the back corner. I sat back, watching the groupies who were supposed to be waiting on their man watch my brother then look at me and roll their eyes, wishing they had my spot. I laughed, thinking if they only knew. Travis hugged me, then we sat down and he asked, "What you laughing at?"

"Nigga, you got all these groupies in here hating me, and I'm only the li'l sister. How's that?"

He smiled. "Easy, look at me then look at you, we both fly in our own right!"

I laughed. "True! True. But enough of that. What's got you upset and worked up that you're calling me baby girl and dropping the code before we hung up the phone?"

He looked at me with a look of pain, anger, and hurt, then dropped his voice. "Cook fucking my celly. And before you get all worked up, I don't want to just react too fast and loud, I wanna to do something slow and quiet."

He sat there and told me how when she was bringing him his shot, some would be missing, and she'd say "That's all I have here. She would disappear from the tier for hours before I'd see her again. At count time, she avoids eye contact with the nigga and has a nervous look on her face. This nigga would leave off the tier longer than he usually does.

"Baby girl, I been watching the nigga, and it's funny because he thinks he been watching me, but I know something is up and that it's faulty and full of foul play."

I sat there stunned, not knowing what to say because this was really serious shit. My brother must've read my thoughts because he said, "Don't worry because I want you to do what you been doing normally, and don't change the way you are with her. I need them to think I don't know, and when the time comes, Imma take care of both of them."

After we discussed the plan on what route we were gonna take next, he asked me what was bothering me. I told him how I thought Anita's been getting high with her dude the one I told him about and how I'm starting not to trust her.

He said, "Janikka, when your instincts tell you something, listen to it because nine times out of ten, they're never wrong. If I would've listened to mine the day of the robbery, I wouldn't be sitting right here today doing a 13-year bid behind a muthafuckin' snitch that was supposed to be my homie."

I still looked like something was bothering me, so he asked what else was up.

"Travis, I'm thinking about taking li'l Micheal from Anita because I don't feel like she's being a fit mother. She got that nigga in her house smoking crack while my li'l man sits in his room all day!"

"How do you know that, Jay?"

"Because, B.I.G., li'l Micheal told me the other night he always smell something funny when he goes into the kitchen and that he told Anita, but she didn't do nothing."

He leaned back in his seat in deep thought, contemplating his next words. "Baby girl, I don't trust Anita and never have since you brought her here to meet me. I just got a vibe from her that doesn't sit well with me, and I'm telling you now, watch her closely and do what you feel is best for li'l Micheal."

We talked some more about idle stuff when the guard said, "Time's up!" We hugged, and he kissed me on the cheek. Then he told me to watch my back and to remember what he said. I walked out that waiting room with a heavy heart and a lot on my mind. My whole drive back was filled with my brother's voice telling me about Cook and this nigga that's been bunking with him for a little over a year. Bitches were grimy. Just when you think someone is loyal to you, they step outta their role and show their true character. The plan that my brother had would surely work, but there would be someone getting hurt in the process.

As I pulled into my driveway, I saw it was barely turning six o'clock, still kinda early. I don't know if my li'l nigga will be ready to go home yet because him and Darnisha went to the mall and to a movie after. Every time li'l Micheal is with us, we take him to go get new clothes. Imma have a conversation with Darnisha tonight about what she'll think about adopting li'l Micheal because I have a feeling that Anita's been getting high. For the last two weeks, she's always tired and always in a rush to get home. We usually go out after we see a client or on Fridays, but she'd been creating a distance between us, and I can't figure out why.

I walked in the house, and it was quiet, so that meant Darnisha and li'l Micheal were still out, so I walked to the fridge and grabbed me a vodka Smirnoff, popped it open, and walked to the room. I kicked my shoes off, threw my keys on the dresser, and turned the stereo on while I took a shower. I hated it when it's quiet in the house. Before I jumped in the shower, I called Anita's cell phone. She picked up on the second ring.

"Wassup, Anita, what you got going on?"

"Nothing, just walked in the house a little while ago. What time are y'all bringing my baby home?"

"Well, I was calling to let you know that whenever Darnisha and him come back from the mall, we'll drop him off."

It was quiet for a minute, then I heard a sniffle.

"Are you still going to the doctor's tomorrow, and do you still want me to go with you?" I asked.

"Umm, Jay, I don't know what I want. Really, to tell you the truth, I'm going through so much right now. I'm not ready for another child, it's already hard with li'l Micheal."

"Nene, what do you mean it's hard? You make good money at the shop, you're sitting far with all the money the clients bring in when we get them. I don't understand what you mean by hard!"

Anita sighed loudly then replied impatiently, "Janikka, you wouldn't understand what I'm talking about because you haven't walked in my shoes, you're not dealing with a man that don't appreciate shit you do! And you don't have a fucking child to know what it's like, so don't go asking me all these fucking questions and wondering why I'm feeling the way I'm feeling!"

Holding the phone away from my ear, I sat there shocked and stunned at how she just went off. But before I could say anything, she was yelling again. "Jay, I don't need you with me tomorrow. I'm tired of your shit! Just drop my son off, and I'll see you Tuesday or later on in the week when it's business to handle."

Then she hung up the phone. Really sitting there flabbergasted, I shook my head then got up to go take my shower. In the shower, I shook off the illness of the day with the hot, steamy water running down my back, feeling better as I lathered up and rinsed off. When I stepped out the shower, I heard laughter from downstairs. Knowing my babies were home put the first smile on my face all day. I hurried up and put on some Victoria Secret sweats and T-shirt then went downstairs.

"Auntie Jay, we saw the Chipmunks movie, and it was so funny I almost peed my pants," li'l Micheal exclaimed.

"Isn't that right! So that must mean you enjoyed yourself this weekend, right?"

Li'l Micheal walked over to me and hugged me around my waist. "I'm always happy and have a lot of fun when I'm with you and Auntie Nisha. I love you both so much!"

Looking up at Darnisha in the kitchen, I smiled and winked at her.

"All right, li'l man, it's time to get all your stuff together so I can drop you off at home in a little bit. Darnisha, my love, are you riding with me or are you staying home until I get back?" I asked her.

"No, babe, I'll go with you to take li'l daddy. Let me go get his stuff situated while you two talk until you're ready to go."

On the drive back to Anita's spot, we cloned all the way there. We got there so quick I didn't notice the Escalade in the driveway and thought that we passed the house until I looked up. Li'l Micheal was already jumping out the back seat, excited to go see his momma. Me and Darnisha got out carrying his overnight bag and shopping bags from the mall purchases they made today. Anita opened the door with a fake smile at me but grabbed li'l Micheal in a big bear hug then told him to tell us goodbye because he has to get ready for school in the morning. I kissed my li'l man goodbye then turned to Anita and asked whose truck was in her driveway. When she said it's Larnell's, I damn near passed out. Darnisha was already in the car, so I just sat everything by the door and left without another word.

On my and Darnisha's drive back home, I was unusually quiet, so she asked if I was okay.

"I'm fine, baby, why do you ask?"

"I don't know, you're just so quiet, and you look like you're in deep thought."

"Nisha, how would you feel if we kept li'l Micheal and raised him on our own?"

I could tell that she was caught off guard by my question, but I needed an answer from her.

"Jay, I would love that because I love that little boy like he were my own, but I don't think it will ever happen considering that Anita takes good care of her son."

She looked at me when she heard me "Hmph" too loud, so she asked, "Jay, what is this really about?"

"Nothing, Darnisha. You'll know very soon though, my love, you'll know very soon."

Chapter 11

Getting off the table to put back on my clothes, the doctor confirmed that I was indeed six weeks pregnant with a growing baby. I wasn't surprised at all because even between all the arguing me and Larnell do, I liked to have sex every single night. I just didn't know if I'm ready for another child. I wasn't lying when I told Jay that I wasn't ready because I'm seriously not. The doctor walked back in as I was putting on my coat with a prescription of folic acid and prenatal vitamins. I said thank you and walked out of the doctor's office.

Once I got in my car, my cell phone rang. I jumped because it scared me, but once I picked it up and heard the operator then a familiar voice, I smiled.

"Wassup, baby," a baritone voice said through the phone.

"Nothing, just missing you more and more each day."

"Well, you should've thought about that when you felt the need to listen to your little friend."

"Aww, baby, I don't wanna talk about that. Is everything all right with you?"

Every time me and my boo get on the phone, he wanted to remind me why we are now speaking on the phone the way we do instead of being together like we're supposed to.

"Iea, I'm straight, I just wanted to let you know I got everything handled on my end. Just make sure you come up here on Saturday."

"I will. I haven't let you down yet, why would I start now? I love you, always remember that!"

"I will. And I love you too."

After I hung up the phone, I leaned my head back on the headrest before I started up the car. Knowing that I needed to get things situated and clear the air with Jay, I called her cell phone. When she picked up, I blew out a sigh then said, "I'm sorry."

Jay was quiet on the phone a long while before talking. "It's okay. How did the appointment go?" she asked.

"It went fine. I'm still in the parking lot. I just wanted to talk to you because I feel bad for going off the way I did when you did nothing wrong."

"Nene, I'm not trippin' off that. I'm getting used to your mood swings you've been having these last few months, and besides, we go too far back for me to even get all worked up from a spiel over nothing."

Then we both sat there in awkward silence on the phone, me wanting to wait out an answer for her next question and her worrying about how she's going to ask me. So I just cleared my throat and said, "Yes, Jay, I'm pregnant again, and I'm six weeks today."

"Oh, I'm so sorry, Anita. Is there anything you need me to do? Do you want me to meet you at our favorite spot for lunch?"

"Yeah, sweetie, meet me at Marissa's in about thirty minutes."

"All right, I'll see you then, and Anita?"

"Yeah?"

"I love you."

"I love you too."

After hanging up the phone, I started my car and started heading toward Marissa's. Janikka just didn't know what I have in store for her future. She thought that her world was so perfect right now. I couldn't wait until it just starts crashing down! She thought that I was grateful for her calling the police that night she walked in and saw that Micheal beating my ass once again. I was miserable, and these past three years apart have been even worse. I wouldn't be with Larnell if it weren't for Jay. My life had been spiraling down with li'l Micheal, the only good part in it, and now it's time for Jay to feel the same way I felt when she snatched away my love, my world, my everything. I was so engrossed in my revenge on my best friend that I didn't see her pulling up behind me in the parking lot at Marissa's.

She hopped out her car, and I plastered on a smile of contentment until the time comes. We walked arm in arm inside the restaurant to our favorite table in the back. Once seated, the waitress took our orders and placed our drinks on the table. When the waitress was out of earshot, we started our conversation.

Jay said, "Well, did you think about what you're gonna do and how you gonna tell Larnell?"

"To be honest with you, I haven't really thought about it, I mean I'm only six weeks today. So if I do decide to abort it, I have time."

She didn't speak for a minute, and I could tell that she was pondering her words and thoughts. "That's fine, Anita. Just know that whatever decision you make, Imma back you up and be there for you 100 percent. But since we're here, I need to discuss two things with you."

"Which is?"

"Well, one is Darnisha party that I'm planning for next Friday night at the House of Blues."

"Oh, Jay, that's wassup. What is it you're gonna need for me to do?"

"I'm only gonna need you to get the word out to family and friends that we're having a birthday party and that they can invite a friend or two."

"Okay, that's it? You don't need me to do nothing else?"

"Naw! And second we need to stop at the office after this because we have a meeting next Wednesday, and I need you to be ready. That's if you're still on duty."

I sat there thinking for a minute about who was supposed to be the next client but really couldn't come up with nothing.

"Yeah, you know we're still on!"

The waitress came with our candida wet burritos, Ceviche with tortilla chips freshly fried with tortilla shells, and a side order of extra cilantro. Me and Jay were in silence, loving the way this place made their burritos. We'd been going here for years just for their top rate wet burritos. After we ate, we both passed on dessert, paid the waiter, and made our exit. Back in the parking lot, we agreed to meet at the office tonight at eight o'clock. I drove straight home because Larnell said that he would pick up Junior.

When I got there, I unlocked the door as fast as I could and rushed upstairs because I had a little time to feed my nose, cook dinner, and get ready to go back out to meet Jay. After I tooted about three lines, I rolled me up a blunt to mellow out my high. I turned my stereo on then headed to the kitchen. I pulled out some pork chops, mashed potatoes, corn, and some brownie mix to make my baby some dessert after dinner. While I let the pork chops stall out, I went to quickly jump in and out the shower. When Larnell and li'l Micheal walked in the house, I was in front of the stove in my long silk robe turning over the last of the pork chops.

"Mommy. Mommy, what you doin'?"

I turned to go pick up my little man and kissed his cheeks then said, "I'm cooking dinner for you, my sweetie pie, so why don't you go in the room, take off your school clothes, then head to the bathroom to wash your hands before coming to eat your food?"

Scrambling to get out of my arms, he said, "Okay, Mommy."

Li'l Micheal ran to his room to get himself ready for dinner. Larnell walked up to me and wrapped his arms around my waist while I was at the stove. He kissed my ear then whispered, "I hope I get dessert, too, tonight."

I leaned my head back to kiss him on the lips and felt his hardness through the jeans he had on.

"Yeah, you'll get dessert when I come back from hooking up with Janikka tonight. We have some important things to go over concerning an upcoming meeting with a client later on this week."

I felt his body tense up, so I knew that he was getting upset because I was leaving back out tonight. Then he went in by grabbing me by my neck and hissed out, "How long do I have to go through this shit, Anita? You leave almost every night, then every Saturday morning you at meeting all the time. Tell me this, is there really any fucking meetings!"

Surprised that this nigga was throwing allegations my way and accusing me of cheating, it took me longer than usual to answer, and he tightened his grasp on the back of my neck.

"Babe, I-I-I swear it's meeting, and everything I do is for us," I said, trembling.

Before Larnell could reply back to what I was saying, li'l Micheal ran back into the kitchen. He quickly let go of my neck and leaned in to kiss my cheek then whispered in my ear again, telling me that we'd finish it later. Happy that my son walked in, I quickly straightened my face and turned the stove off. After I took the brownies out of the oven, I made their plates. Larnell was already in the back room probably getting high, so I sat his plate in the microwave.

I sat down at the table with my son and talked to him about his school day until he was finished with his food.

"Mommy, can I have some brownies now?" li'l Micheal asked.

"No, baby, they have to cool off, so Imma take you a bath first. Then Imma give you a few brownies, and then Mommy has to go somewhere with Auntie Jay, so I won't be able to tuck you in tonight."

"K, Mommy, I'm ready to take my bath now!"

After I washed him up with soap real good, I let him play with his planes and cars for a while. I went in the room to get dressed and saw Larnell's eyes glazed over while he was laying on the bed, focused on something on his jeans. Seeing that he was on stuck, I hurried up to let him know that his food was in the microwave and that li'l Micheal was in his room watching TV until it was time for him to go to bed. He didn't answer and just waved me off. I walked to li'l Micheal's room, kissed him good night, then headed out the door to go meet Jay at the office.

Chapter 12

When I went to go see my boo that weekend on Saturday like I do every weekend, I told him about me and Jay's client that we were planning on getting at later on tonight. My boo knows about my situation I got going on with Janikka and this client shit. In fact, he encouraged me to get with it because at first I wasn't really feeling the stick-up kid shit. The only reason why I knew how to handle a gun was because my pops was an ex-marine office, and he had them all over the house before he and my mother died in a car crash eight years ago.

He wanted a son so bad but only had my son. He always was rough with me and had me doing outdoor stuff that I wasn't really into. But seeing that my boo looked at anything I did with Janikka as opportunities for the future, he made me see the possibilities I could form by getting involved. So sitting across the table on Saturday in the visiting room telling him about the Mexican dude Rick we were about to get for his jewelry, he came up with the perfect plan to spook Janikka and somewhat have her paranoid in the near future.

I told him that I didn't know how it was supposed to work or how I was gonna set it up, knowing that Rick told her, he was going to be alone. He then gave me this dude's name's, Laman, number and told me to call him and tell him the time and place, and he'll handle everything else from there. I said okay and trusted him to take care of the rest.

After Janikka came to pick me up from the house, we drove out to this vacant little fame place where Rick told us to meet him. It was dark out, but we did the look around to see it was a car that I parked behind the barn, a white picket fence, all dirt and field surrounded. We were gonna go in there as is because the dude was by himself and liked to see who he did business with. I was supposed to wait until Rick showed the jewelry and Jay showed the cash before I dropped his body. She told me to make sure that I didn't look suspicious or the whole situation was gonna fuck up.

After Jay checked to make sure the money was stacked nice in the briefcase and her gun was at her ankle, she grabbed the briefcase out the back seat, turned to me to see if I was good and ready with my silencer screwed on my Desert Eagle, one shagged on my side and the other in my back underneath the old UCLA college hoodies I had on so it won't look so bulky and obvious.

We stepped out the car and did another look around before we started approaching the barn door. I wasn't into walking inside a trap, and Jay wasn't either. When we stepped inside the barn, it had hat and cages everywhere. Birds were flipping out in cages to the left and right of us. It was a park-looking wooden table in the middle of the floor with bird shit all on top. The place reeked of horse shit. Me and Jay both covered our noses at the same time. When we looked at each other to say something, what sounded like a door creaked open. We both looked at the way we came in and didn't see anybody, but then we heard a voice coming from what looked like the back of the barn but was actually a back door saying, "Welcome, ladies, sorry about the smell."

Looking at Rick with the case in his hand and sunglasses on, I just wanted to get the whole thing over with and was wondering where the hell Lamar and his homie was because it stank in here. Janikka started talking while I stood off to the side.

"Wassup, Rick! Here, man, let's hurry up because I don't want this shitty smell lingering on my clothes," she walked toward the table, set the briefcase down, and opened it up.

"Aww, my lady, always about her business, that's what I love about you, senorita." He looked over at me then nodded his head and said, "So this the friend you told me about, I assume?"

Looking back at me, Janikka said, "Yeah, that's her. My other half, now can we do this because it stinks."

Laughing, he seemed to have relaxed and put his briefcase on the table. When he opened it up, he stepped back. "Go ahead, senora, pick whatever you like. I have—" and before he could finish the sentence, he must've seen me pull out because he reached for his pistol behind his back, but it was too late because I dropped him before he had the chance.

As soon as Janikka poured all the jewelry out of his briefcase into hers and closed it, shot rang out. Janikka grabbed the case and dropped behind one of the cages, and I dropped behind the other.

Jay screamed out "What the fuck!" and started shooting back.

Bullets were flying back and forth with hay flying and birds screams stopping in midchirp. I saw Janikka scramble to the front of the door and push it open with her foot, and she signaled for me to come on and to stay low. When the bullets seized for a minute, knowing they were reloading, we took our chance to get out alive.

We both let out a few more rounds and got out of that barn as quick as possible.

When we closed the door, she started reversing the car out of there, the back window got hit when we turned the car around. I leaned out the front seat firing back when the two sides ran back in the barn.

Janikka was in the car going off when I pulled myself back into the seat. "What the fuck! Damn, Nene, that muthafucka set us up! We could've been killed back there. Fuck!" she screamed again and hit the steering wheel.

I replied, "Calm down, Jay, we out of there. Let's just get somewhere safe where we could calm down and have a drink."

"You're right, you're right. I just hope we don't get pulled over for that window before we make it downtown."

We drove all the way back downtown in silence, lost in thought. I was thinking, *How the fuck did Lamar and his homie get in that barn without us seeing?* Well, it doesn't even matter, my boo said that he was gonna take care of it, and he did because I could see that Janikka was shook the fuck up!

Chapter 13

It was Darnisha's big night, and I was determined not to let my fucked-up week ruin what I've been planning for my baby for almost three weeks. As I stepped out the shower and into the bedroom, I shook my thoughts away from what happened on Wednesday night with Rick. I just couldn't get past how we and Anita almost lost our life. Right when Rick's body dropped and I went to grab the briefcase, bullets started flying. A bullet went right past my ear.

Our problem now was that we left people alive that could have seen us and were looking for us right now.

I snapped out of my trance and noticed that Darnisha had walked in looking like a top model on a runway. She was rocking the birthday fit I bought her yesterday, knowing she was killing the game with a purple strapless dress cut off above the knee. She walked over to me and kissed my lips, asking why I looked so spaced out.

"Naw, baby, I'm good. I'm just having second thoughts on going to this party, and instead, maybe I should keep you all to myself right here in the house and go round for round like we did this morning."

"Baby, we can't do that even though I would love it. You said your friend wanted you to go as a VIP guest, so we're going even though it's my birthday. Now why aren't you dressed, sweetie? Are you okay for real? You've been very distant for the past couple days."

"I'm fine, my love. I'm getting dressed now because the limo should be here in about fifteen minutes, are you ready?"

"Yeah, I just got to put on my eyeliner and mascara and then I'm good to go."

As Darnisha applied her minimal makeup, I got dressed rapidly, knowing the limo would be here and that the partygoers were expecting us to walk in the House of Blues at 11:00 p.m. When the limo pulled up and called to let us know that they were downstairs, I set the alarm and grabbed her purple and gold clutch purse, and we were out and ready to enjoy the rest of our night.

When we pulled up to the club, the normal club goers were standing outside, trying to figure out why they had to wait to enter the club. Before we stepped out the limo, the bouncers rolled out the red carpet like they were paid to do. When I stepped out in my charcoal gray, knee-length, short, gray blazer and a violet purple dress blouse underneath, with a simple gold necklace full of diamonds, a pair of studded gold earrings, my hair straight down and with some gray-and-purple pump, I had everyone's attention.

But when I reached my hand out to pull Darnisha out the car, everybody's mouth dropped. One because we were a lesbian couple, and two because we represented long money and the reason why they were still standing outside of the club.

Once the driver closed the door, we proceeded to walk the carpet to the front door. When it opened, Darnisha got the shock of her life. Everyone screamed "Happy birthday!" and confetti dropped, and her daddy handed her a champagne flute with a single white rose, compliments of me.

Inside the House of Blues, it was more of a laid-back type of setting with lounge chairs lined up along the walls. There was a bar right in the middle that stretched for about fifteen feet along with about thirty barstools in front of it. They had a VIP section with a few tables, a dance floor, and a bathroom. That pretty much made up the House of Blues and that's why I chose the place. Only a few club goers would be allowed in until they reached capacity because more than half the club was filled up with family and friends.

I had her favorite song "Happy People" by R. Kelly playing while she was being embraced with compliments, hugs, and happy birthdays from friends, family, and colleagues. She turned to me and mouthed "Imma get you," but before I could respond, I caught a glimpse somebody familiar out of the corner of my eye, and to not think I was trippin', I looked. Now knowing I'm not trippin', I saw Toya in the corner with some broad. *What was she doing here?* I thought to myself when Anita walked up and said, "The bouncers wanna know if they can let the people in now."

"Yeah, but, Nene, what is Toya doing here? Who invited her?" I asked.

She just looked at me and shrugged then walked off. I brushed it off because as long as she didn't fuck up my baby's night, I'm good. If only I knew how good it would actually be.

*****

As I was walking to let the bouncers know it was cool to start letting people in, I was chuckling to myself. It was a good thing that I did invite Toya because I would've been bored outta my mind without knowing something was gonna pop off. Knowing Toya, I knew she was gonna want to take out Jay sometime tonight because she's sprung like that for some reason. As soon as she did, I would send Darnisha right to them on accident, of course, and I couldn't wait to see Jay's slick ass get out of being caught red-handed with one of her exes at her woman's party. Laughing, I turned my attention to the bouncer. "Let them in now."

I continued my walk to the bathroom to refresh my nose before I joined everybody at the table. I had to have some type of encouragement to be around Jay, Nisha, and that damn daddy back of hers with his sexy ass. I wondered if he'd fuck me good like he'd been doing that young girlfriend of his…

*****

"What, Toya, damn! You been giving me the eye all night, and it's my bitch birthday!"

Smiling and pulling at my blazer, she said, "I know, but you're lookin' good tonight, and who cares about her when you been looking at me the same way I been looking at you?"

She had a point there because that's why I was in the bathroom with her. She was looking good in one of those Chanel spaghetti

67

strapped dresses that accentuated her every curve. My eyes had been following her ass all night, wondering if she had any panties on.

Now in this stall, I finally put my hand under her dress to find that she didn't have any panties on and was soaking wet for me. I pushed her up against the stall door and pushed my two fingers deep inside her while I stifled her moan with my mouth. I went to town with my fingers while massaging her clit with my thumb, pushing my index and middle finger inside her so she could cum fast and I could get the fuck outta there before Darnisha thought I was missing for too long. She hadn't noticed Toya's presence at the club yet because there were too many people and the plentiful drinking helped blur her vision…hopefully.

But I knew I had to hurry up and get rid of her before Toya made herself visible. She was crazy like that if I didn't show her a little attention, and trust me, she wasn't making it easy for me to avoid her. First by dancing with the woman I saw her with earlier then by brushing up against me and grabbing my ass every chance she had. When I felt my fingers being coated with her juices, I pulled them out, kissed her again, then told her to clean herself.

As luck was on my side, as soon as I stepped to the sink to wash my hands, Darnisha walked in the restroom smiling and sounding extra chippery when she said, "Baby, what's taking so long? Anita been looking for you, and I told her you went to the bathroom, and it seemed like you fell in."

Laughing at her own joke, I cleared my throat, grabbed a napkin. "Naw, I'm cool, just had to use the bathroom that's all. Let's go dance, baby!"

As we were about to walk out the bathroom, the stall door pushed open, and Darnisha turned around to see Toya walking toward the sink. Darnisha looked at me then looked at Toya and said, "Bitch! What the fuck you doing here at my party?"

Toya cleared her throat and looked around before looking back at Darnisha. "I know you not talking to me because I'm clearly not the bitch in this bathroom you're referring to." She rolled her eyes and smacked her lips, "And to answer your question, I was invited, and if I would've known it was your birthday party, I would've never come."

When Darnisha started walking toward her, I grabbed her by the waist and pulled her back. "Calm down, babe!"

She turned on me and yelled, "Calm down? This bitch at my muthafuckin' party, and when I come looking for you, you and this bitch is in the bathroom together!"

I whispered in her ear, "Don't jump to conclusions, I didn't know she was in here."

Obviously, Darnisha didn't give a fuck about what I was saying and tried rushing at Toya again. Toya started laughing and said, "Yeah, Jay, you better get her because this time she not gonna be so lucky!"

Before Darnisha could say anything, I looked at Toya and said, "All right, that's enough now. Get out and don't let me see you when we come out this bathroom."

Toya looked me up and down, licked her lips, then looked at Darnisha with a smirk and said, "Yeah, whatever you say." Looking back at Darnisha, she said, "Don't let me catch you, bitch."

I yelled "That's enough!" and Toya walked out the door. When she did, I walked to the sink, and Danisha was right on my heels. I turned around, and she slapped the shit out of me. I grabbed her by the wrist.

"Darnisha, what I tell you about you're muthfuckin' hands!"

Ignoring what the fuck I was saying, she screamed, "So you gonna fuck your ex on my birthday in a fucking bathroom. Are you serious?" Then she started swinging on me again.

Grabbing ahold of her wrist once again, I said, "I didn't fuck her, and I didn't know she was in here!"

"Whatever, Jay, your ass is always doing some sneaky shit. As soon as I start to trust you, your ass is back to fucking around on me. What the fuck!"

I tried hugging her, and she pushed me back. "NO! Don't fucking touch me. Thanks for a good birthday party." She stormed out the bathroom.

"Fuck!" I screamed to myself and straightened out my blazer, knowing this was gonna be a long fucking night and hoping Toya left the club like I told her to.

Back out in the club, Darnisha wouldn't look at me or get close to me. Richard noticed the vibe but didn't comment on it. I sat back and watched Darnisha toss back drink after drink while she was scanning the room as if looking for a victim. Anita walked up to me while I was watching Darnisha, sat down, and started talking and asking me questions.

"What happened in there?" she asked.

"Nothing. Toya was coming out on of the stalls when we were about to leave out."

She blew out a low whistle. "Word! Damn, that's some shit. If I knew you was in there getting it in, I would've never told her I was looking for you. Where Toya at now?"

"I don't know, I told her—" and before I could finish my sentence, I heard yelling from the middle of the dance floor.

When me and Anita started walking toward the crowd, I heard Toya's voice screaming, "LET GO MY HAIR, BITCH!"

I started running, trying to get to the ruckus as fast as I could. By the time I got there, one security had Darnisha by the waist with her legs and arms wailing, still screaming, "IMMA KILL YOU, BITCH! STAY AWAY FROM MINES!"

Another had Toya by the arm while she yelled "This ain't over, bitch!" and trying to fix herself while they were escorting her out the club.

I went over to Darnisha, mad I let Anita distract me from watching her and letting her out of my sight. When the security had her in VIP, he finally set her down.

I walked over and asked, "What the fuck happened, Nisha?"

She started yelling, "Don't fucking ask me what happened. You the one fuckin' bitches in the bathroom on muthafuckin' birthday!"

Noticing that people were watching us and that we had everybody's attention, I gave her a deadly don't-fuck-with-me look. "Go get your shit, and let's go, Darnisha. We'll finish this at home." She didn't move. I got closer to her and said it again, "Get yo shit and let's go before I embarrass yo ass and drag you out this club!"

Darnisha got up, fixed her dress, walked over to her dad, kissed his cheek, hugged his girlfriend goodbye, and headed for the exit. I thanked everybody for coming and to enjoy the rest of their night.

Out in front while we waited for the limo, Darnisha stood a good distance away from me. That was good because I was liable to knock her upside her damn head for embarrassing me and herself in that club. When the limo pulled up and we got in the back seat, Darnisha said, "How the fuck you gonna be mad at me when you're little girlfriend started the shit?"

"That ain't my little nothing, and why the fuck did you have to start fighting and shit in the fucking club! That shit is embarrassing. Now I gotta pay for the inconvenience and disturbance you caused."

She smacked her lips and rolled her eyes. "What the fuck ever, Jay, I'm so sick of your shit."

I screamed, "Good because I'm sick of you too with your insecure ass!"

We didn't say nothing else to each other for the rest of the drive all the way home. Man, this was turning out to be one long-ass night, with more to go.

*****

Standing in the back corner talking to Larnell, I watched Toya came out the bathroom with a smirk on her face. Knowing Darnisha must've seen them together put a smile on my face.

Mission complete.

Janika's ass got caught red-handed just like I wanted her to, but knowing how dumb these bitches were over her, this incident didn't curb my appetite one bit. So little after Darnisha and Jay came out, I went to go try to find out what happened and get the whole story behind that smirk Toya had on her face. The bitches started fighting. Now that's what I call a little bit of action, and from where I was standing, it looked like Darnisha was whoopin' the shit out of Toya's little ass. Toya ain't a comparison matched up with Darnisha; even though Toya could fight, Darnisha learned how to throw them fists from somewhere!

After Jay and Darnisha walked out the club to go home, I went back over to Larnell, asking him if he was ready to go because I was horny as fuck. I needed to freshen up my nose and didn't have any more on hand, so I was more than happy to leave. On our drive home I was thinking about the next little inconvenient situation I was planning to put in Janikka's path. Smiling at the fight again and fully satisfied on how the night turned out, I laid my head back and smiled all the way home.

Chapter 14

These last couple of weeks have been long and full of paranoia for me. I've been feeling like somebody's watching me, and I even saw a couple of cars following me more than once. Toya had been getting on my nerves, wanting to see me every day, and if that's not it, she's blowing up my damn phone nonstop with a blocked number at different hours in the night. I knew it was her because Toya was the only broad I've been fucking besides my woman. I knew I should've cut her ass off after that whole incident at the club, but the pussy was good and she served her purpose when I don't wanna be bothered with Darnisha, so I deal with her stupid shit.

Then on top of all that, Anita was now strung out on drugs and flippin' out every chance she gets. It's getting bad, and it's to the point where she's getting high at the shop. I went to her office the other week to talk to her about me being followed earlier that day only to walk in and see her head tilted back. I guess she was enjoying the drip, but when she noticed I walked in, she swiped at her nose for the residue of the white substance left at the tip of her nose. I just ignored the whole situation and spoke on what I went to talk to her about then left without ever saying a word about her drug of choice.

I'm sure by now that she knew that I knew she's getting high, but since I'm not saying anything, she felt that she didn't have to say anything. Just last weekend when I went to go pick up li'l Micheal, me and Larnell got into an argument because his punk ass said something slick about bitches sucking on each other's pussies around his son. I totally flipped and cussed his ass out from here all the way back to the Garden of Eden, and what made matter worse, Anita's stupid ass gonna take his side over mine by asking me to leave before she ended up saying something that nigga smoking up all her money while she sniffing it up, and she's gonna tell me to leave before she said something. So things between Anita and I had been cordial because of li'l Micheal, but I can't stand her ass right now.

I hated that I have to stop by her office before I make a run to my office in Long Beach, but I needed her to know a few things before I left for the day because I didn't plan on coming back in, so I took a deep breath then knocked on her office door. Ever since the last time, I now knock before entering.

She said, "Come in."

I turned the knob. Walking in, she nodded and gestured for me to sit down. When I sat down, I asked, "So how much does Tony owe?"

Anita looked down at the document that recorded all the barbers and beauticians' booth fee payments.

"She owes $1,000, and out of the past three months, she's only paid $800 in total."

Sitting back going over the information just given to me in my head, I quickly added three months' worth of booth fees which would be a total of $1,800, that means I'm losing out on a lot of money, and I can't have to, so I asked, "Well, when you asked her about the money and why she's late, what did she say?"

"Well, she said that she was backed up on her rent last month and the month before last and that she hadn't really been having clients last month, so she couldn't pay off this month's yet. Then I told her I'd put her on a weekly fee until she caught up, but that was two months ago when she was late the first time. And she's been paying, that's how she paid the $800 so far, but for the last two weeks, she hasn't been giving me nothing and always have a story when we talk."

Anita started shaking her head then said, "That's why I put that note on your desk to ask you to speak with her or tell me how you want me to handle it."

I grabbed the file off Anita's desk and reread what she already told me and shook my head. "I guess she no longer has a booth. Tell her that she can keep the money she owes me. Clean her locker and booth area, drop off her locker key, and leave my shop. I can't tolerate her lying to use on why she can't pay her rent fee, homegirl or not. When I see clients in her chair every day, I also can't tolerate the fact that even after you tried to work out a deal with her, she still isn't paying on time. So she's fired and kicked out the shop. You can start looking for a replacement immediately so we don't have an idle booth for long."

"All right, Jay, I'll let her know before I close up the shop when everyone's leaving just in case she makes a scene."

"That's fine, but before I leave, I'm just letting you know I'm not coming back before closing time. I have to swing by the office because I got a buyer for another one of those things, and I'll have something for you tomorrow. If you need anything, hit me up on my phone."

I got up to leave then walked to my office to grab my things and headed out the shop.

*****

After Janikka left out my office and out the shop, I reached for the phone to call Larnell to let him know it was time for him to put that plan in motion because today was the day. Larnell had a different beef with Janikka than mine. One night when he was talking shit about her, I asked him why he hated her so much. Then he told me about a time when he was robbed for the last of his shit and got up money by her brother, Travis, about seven years ago before Travis went to prison. And that's when he first met Janikka. He didn't know that was the dude's sister until he overheard a conversation me and her were having about visiting him a while back. Then I asked him if that shit happened years ago, why he still got beef about it? Then he told me that, that money was all that he had left to his name and that he was on a come up after just hitting a lick.

Then after he got robbed, he didn't have nowhere to go or a place to stay and ended up staying with an old head that got him smoking crack. And even though he was smoking, he was functional and had been robbing little heist to get high, clothe himself, and pay the rent. He said that he was never able to come in contact with enough money because he was hiding from the muthfuckaz he robbed to even have that getup money in the first place.

That same night, I told him that I didn't really care for her the way she thinks I do, but I didn't tell him why and he didn't ask because he was too focused on me telling him how I knew a way we could get Travis back through her and how he could come in contact with way more than he lost. But the only thing and most important was he couldn't kill her or let her see his face and to get in and get out. I just hoped that everything goes as planned. I put my feet up, looked in my purse for my compact filled with goodies, and tooted my nose with a smile on my face while I waited for Larnell to call me back to let me know that the deed was done!

*****

On my drive downtown, I thought about Tony. I hated to fire her, but I can't have anybody working for me that couldn't pay. Now I don't know what the real problem is, but I knew for sure that she was having clients in her chair back-to-back. Maybe she's getting high on something, who knows? I couldn't be for certain of too much on anything nowadays with all the bullshit and drama going on in my life.

I don't even know who my best friend was anymore. She's gettin' high like it's going outta style, and she's done choosing her nigga over our relationship. Where they do that faulty shit at? Nowadays, it looked like everywhere!

Then my thoughts fell back on Darnisha and Toya. I've been seeing a lot of Toya lately. She's done leaving that stripper chick, Diamond I think her name was, alone just to be back with me. And as Toya put it, the chick was not too happy with that and been blowing Toya's phone up constantly. Then Darnisha was back to calling my phone back-to-back, every hour on the hour, on something like I-need-to-know-your-every-move-stalker type shit. I swear I'm getting fed up with these bitches!

After doubling around the block a couple of times and constantly checking my rearview mirror, I pulled up in the driveway. Taking the office keys out of my glove compartment, I cut the engine off and stepped out the car. Looking at the time and seeing that it was only four o'clock, I guess I'll hurry up so I could surprise Darnisha and take her out to dinner tonight. Walking toward the house, I felt that rumbling feeling inside my stomach that I'd been feeling all day. Ignoring it like I'd also been doing all day, I continued up the porch.

I turned to see the neighbor's cat purring at the front door and no car in the driveway. I knew that they weren't home. Aww, sorry, kitty! Then a thought popped in my head that made me smile; Imma get Darnisha a puppy or kitty cat, li'l Micheal would love that. After I put the key in the door and turned the knob, I felt a foot kick me in my ass and flew me forward, face first.

"What the fuck!" I screamed as I was tryna lift myself up.

I didn't even hear anybody run up on me. I was forced right back down with another kick and a gruesome "Shut up, bitch!"

I felt myself being dragged then punched and kicked before I passed out...

*****

Trying to open my eyes in this dark room, I tried to remember what happened. I couldn't feel my legs, my stomach felt like it was wrapped around my spine. I lifted my hand up to feel my lips, and they're swollen and feeling like the biggest things on my face. I wondered why I couldn't open my eye all the way because when I did, it felt half closed.

Then I remembered being pushed inside the door and onto the ground. I remembered somebody grabbing me and dragging me somewhere. I remembered being punched and kicked until I wasn't aware of my surroundings. Then before I was completely out cold, I heard what sounded like someone saying "Look at all this! We hit the muthafucking jackpot!"

When I tried to sit up, I winced because it felt like somebody just kicked me in my ribs. I tried to stand but fell right back on my ass. I took a few deep breaths and tried to stand again with one hand resting on the couch arm. With one arm holding the wall for balance and the other on my stomach as if I needed to hold my guts in place, I walked toward the back room.

I didn't have to go all the way inside the room because the door was wide open, and I could see the safe open and all the drawers emptied out and scattered on the floor.

I couldn't fucking believe that shit! Somebody caught me slippin'. I walked back toward the front, felt my pockets for my keys, and left everything as it was when I walked out the house. When I got in my car, I called Darnisha and told her to meet me at the emergency room and hung up before she could ask any questions. I drove myself all the way to the hospital, and no longer able to endure the sharp pains in my side, I passed out at the entrance.

Chapter 15

Sitting at home stuck in the house these past few days had me thinking and overanalyzing everybody in my life. It'd been too much weird shit going on that I wasn't understanding. After coming back from the hospital and telling Darnisha some lame-ass lie about me getting jumped at the gas station over on Pacific and PCH by some people, a dude and a few females who pushed up on me, gangbanging and asking me to give up my shit. After I told them no, they just started whopping my ass and that the only thing I remember was calling her and somebody driving me to the hospital before passing out.

I told Darnisha not to let anybody know what happened and that I was home because I was gonna tell people I'm out of town. Then she asked why lie, and I said because I don't want people to fucking know. After I screamed at her, she left the situation alone. When Anita called yesterday and asked why I hadn't been at the shop or called her, I told her an emergency came up and that I had to take care of something in San Bernardino and my bad for not calling and to take care of things while I'm gone. I just ignored Toya's calls all together. The only person besides Darnisha I talked to was Travis, and that was because I was supposed to have my little guy hit Cook off with the situations but never got around to it because of the little mishap I encountered. I couldn't tell my B.I.G. what happened over the phone, so I just told him to stand down a few weeks because something came up and I'd come see him in a few weeks also.

I couldn't let him see me like this. I had a fractured rib, black eye, swollen lip, and a bruised hip bone. I was lucky to make it to the hospital without passing out on the road. The doctor told me to take it easy and that in a few weeks I'd be back to normal. Now I'd been trying to place the voice I heard because I knew it. It sounded so familiar. I knew only four people that knew about that house downtown, and I also knew it could've been Rick's dudes getting back at me and finally found the right time. But I was wondering why the robbers didn't kill me. It had to be an inside job. I knew it was a set up. I just didn't know by whom! And until I found out, everybody was a fucking possible suspect. That's why I couldn't tell anybody what happened to me just yet. I took a big loss getting robbed for all that shit in the house. Everything was gone, guns, money, and the jewelry we just came up on. When I find out who did this shit to me, it's gonna be all bad!

*****

"Damn, Larnell! I have to fucking go. I'm already running late, I'm not about to be going through this shit with you."

"For real, it's like that? A nigga just want some pussy, and you telling and shit because you rushing off to some nigga in the penitentiary."

Standing up and walking toward the door, I stopped in my tracks and turned to face him. When I looked at his face, he had this silly smirk just plastered on it. Then he laughed and said, "I knew you didn't think I knew what the fuck you been up to. Every Saturday going up there to go see God knows who. But tell me this, how long have you been keeping those visits a secret?"

Then he crossed his arms and said, "I wonder, does Jay knew that Tashanda opens the shop for you every Saturday?" He was smiling.

He said, "Yeah, I know that too! Now are you gonna give me some pussy, or is it fresh for the nigga you visiting?"

After that, something in me snapped because this muthafucka really didn't know who the fuck he;s fucking with. I screamed at him, seething hot and nose flaring, "You know what, muthafucka, you're right about everything you just fucking said, and I don't give a fuck because you wanna know an ugly truth you seem to forget when you talking to me! HUH?" I paused for a moment before continuing, "Well, let me inform you, I take care of your no-job having, crack-smoking, lazy-ass sorry excuse of a man. I pay rent here! ME!

Not you! I bought your car fresh off the lot with the pink slip and all, and guess what else, muthafucka, I support yo muthfucking drug habit! So what I do is my damn business, and I will continue doing my damn business!"

Before I even could back away, Larnell walked up and slapped the shit outta me and said, "Don't you ever in your fucking life talk to me like that, bitch!"

And before he could say another word, I had my chrome 40 Glock locked and loaded pressed at his temple. I spoke very calmly. "Now, this will be the last time you put yo fucking hands on me. Just because I love you don't mean I won't kill you. Now Imma tell you this one more time, what I do is my business, and there will be no more question about it unless you wanna get your shit and leave. But be sure to leave my muthafucking car!"

While Larnell stood there frozen and in shock, I put my shit back in my purse and walked out the house.

After I reversed out the driveway, I let the tears fall and instantly had a flashback to the night of Micheal's arrest. Micheal had just come home from being out all night, so I was very mad and pissed off that I had to sleep alone again with only Micheal Jr. for comfort. When he walked into our bedroom, I instantly started yelling, "Where the fuck have you been all night, Micheal!"

"Taking care of business."

"I'm tired of yo ass saying the same shit. I'm not fucking stupid, muthafucka. I know you're not taking care of business every night!"

"Anita, I'm tired! I don't have time for this shit. I'm out!"

When he started putting back on his shoes, I hopped off the bed and slapped the shit outta him then started pounding on his chest screaming, "I'm tired of yo shit! I'm so fucking tired. Who is she? Is that where you tryin' to go? Back to your bitch house while me and your son sleep alone in this house without you!"

He grabbed me by the arms and tossed me to the bed and said, "You finished? Huh? I'll be back when your ass cools off." And he started walking.

I scrambled to the bottom drawer crying and pulled out his 9mm handgun he always kept here for emergencies. When I cocked it back and told him that he wasn't going anywhere, he turned around with fire in his eyes. My hand started trembling on the gun because I never seen Micheal this mad.

He charged at me telling, "You wanna pull a gun on me, bitch, like you a man! Imma teach you how to be a man!"

He attacked me, and I dropped the gun. He started hitting me everywhere. I tried fighting back, but that didn't work, he kept pounding and yelling. Yelling and pounding. He wouldn't stop until I felt like I couldn't breathe. When he finally stopped, I was going in and out of consciousness. I heard him walk out the door. I grabbed the phone and called Janikka, and when she answered, I said "Help me!" then passed out.

I didn't know how long it took for her to come over, but when I woke up, I was in the hospital room. Janikka was sitting in a chair next to me with li'l Micheal in her lap and immediately started saying, "I called the police, filed a report, and you're gonna press charges. I'm gonna be a witness, Anita, you can't keep allowing him to do this. When I walked in your house, li'l Micheal was crying, and you were passed out on the bed in your room."

I lay there silently with tears flowing down my face because this time it was really all my fault. Then I dozed back off. When I woke up again, the police were by my side and told me that they had a Micheal Thorton in custody for spousal abuse, domestic violence, possession of a firearm, and two ounces of cocaine with intent to sell. All I could do was cry instead of answering the cop's questions.

*****

When I pulled up into Ironwood State Prison, I checked myself in the mirror, put my purse in the trunk, and proceeded to go through the search procedure before visiting. Ever since Micheal's incarceration, I've been with him every step of the way. It was Micheal's idea for me to stay as Jay's friend and set her up to destroy her. Micheal was first housed in Delano until I told him about Travis and all the information I knew about Jay making sure her brother was getting paid from the inside. Then he figured out how to get transferred and how he could devise a plan from the inside. Micheal hated Janikka and always had. I love Micheal too much to just let him set and do time when it was my fault.

Now every time I walk into this visiting room, it broke my heart to know my one true love isn't walking out with me, but he promised that he would be coming sooner than planned, so I just hoped for the best. As I walked through the visitor's door and sat at my regular table, all I could think about was the baby growing inside me and the fact that I have to abort another one of me and Micheal's children. Janikka thought that I never told Larnell about the first abortion because I didn't want to, but in reality, I didn't tell him because the baby wasn't his.

Larnell can't have children. I was pregnant by Micheal as I am again because every weekend, besides when I'm on my period, we get it in between the vending machines. Remembering the last time we were in between those machines instantly made my pussy wet, and I plastered a smile on my face when a baritone voice said, "What you smiling like that for, sexy?"

I stood up to give my boo a hug, licked his ear, and said, "Because I was just thinking about last weekend when I was here. N-n-n-nasty! Nasty jazz!"

"Oh, if that's the case, I'll be sure to put an even bigger smile on your face before you leave today."

Smiling, I said, "That's wassup, but how are you doing, my love?"

"I'm good, sweetheart, just can't wait to see daylight and little man again. I swear being here makes me realize how much I love the both of you."

"Aww, baby, we love you, too, and we miss you so much. I don't know why you don't let me bring him to see you."

He blew out an agitated breath and said, "How many times do we have to go over this? I don't want my son seeing me like this, and seeing how close he and that bitch is, then I won't put it past him to accidentally say he saw daddy, but I'll be home soon. If all work out hopefully, I'll be home in three months…"

I smiled and squealed, "Really, baby! Don't fucking play with me!"

"I'm not playing. All the ducks are lined up, and I'm going for the kill next week, so just be ready for your man and for that bitch to be behind bars and outta our lives."

We talked about our future plans for most of our visiting time then went to the vending machines to do our do, then I left, feeling like a new woman. By the time I was back on the highway, I was beaming, knowing that my man was coming home soon had me on a high, but I needed to refresh my nose before I went to the shop. Knowing I had to deal with the females then Larnell and li'l Micheal when I got home gave me an instant headache, so I pulled out a freshly rolled blunt, kicked my air conditioner on, put on my Beyoncé 4 CD and enjoyed my ride back to LA.

Chapter 16

Two weeks after I was robbed and beaten, I was able to show my face again. As I walked through the shop, I was greeted like I've been gone for years. I noticed that everything was pretty much the same except for the fact that it was a new girl working at Tony's old booth. She was kinda cute, dark skinned, with some hazel eyes, and when I gave her the quick body scan, I could see that she was shaped in the right areas. I asked her to come to the back later so I could speak to her.

When she was in my office, she seemed kinda shy and left an impression on me. She told me that her name was Miya and that she's been braiding hair since the age of fifteen which would put her skills at eight years' worth of practicing. She didn't have a license and been working from home in her kitchen. I told her that it was nice having her and sent her on her way.

When I went to speak with Anita, she looked bad. She looked as if she lost weight, and she had bags under her eyes. I knew then that I had to talk to her about her habit. So I asked, "Anita, what is it that you're doing because you're losing weight and you look horrible."

She looked at me and said, "Excuse me!"

I gave her the look as if to say "Come on, man, don't play me." She rubbed her temples in a circular motion and said, "Okay, I do a line of coke here and there, but it's nothing major. Just a pick me up after I smoke a blunt."

"Nothing serious!" I said I motioned my arms and swept her body up and down and turned my lip up in disgust and said, "You're dropping weight like a fucking crackhead, and don't you dare lie to me and say it's nothing serious. I've been noticing your sniffling nose, glassy eyes, and snappy attitudes, those are all signs of drug use!"

She threw up her hands and said, "So what? You're judging me now, Jay? You're supposed to be my best friend, not my damn mother!"

My voice was raised to match hers. "I'm your friend! That's why I'm voicing my concern. I'm worried about you and Junior's safety."

With the mention of li'l Micheal, she snapped, pushed back her chair, and raised quickly, "Don't you dare mention my son! Imma damn good mother to my child. Jay, you need to remember that Junior's my son, not yours, because the last time I remembered, you can't have any! Now get the fuck outta my office!"

I stood up quietly and started to walk out then paused at the door, turned around, and said, "It's nice to know how you really feel about me, friend."

Then I closed the door, went to grab my stuff, and left to go meet Toya at her house.

*****

"Hello."

"Where you at, baby?" Darnisha asked on the other end of my cell phone.

I turned toward Toya and put my hands to my lips and told her to be quiet. "On my way home. Why, wassup, is something going on?"

"No, I was just wondering why you wasn't home yet, and it's almost eleven o'clock. This is the third time you've come home late this week."

It seemed like now that every time I talk to Darnisha, I instantly get irritated. I'd been back visiting Toya daily and enjoying every minute of it when she's not blowing up my phone. Other than that, I've been finding myself at her house more than I should be. Toya had left the stripper chick that she was dealing with because I told her that if I'm back in the picture, she can't be with anybody else, no matter what I'm doing. And she happily obliged just so she could have me. As soon as I started telling Darnisha "I told you I've been dealing with a lot of paperwork with the clients and me working on

86

opening another business," I started to tilt my head back because Toya was down there between my legs, flicking her tongue across my clit. I barely heard what Darnisha was saying, so I just cut her off and said, "I'll be home in a minute."

Then I hung up the phone and cut it off. Laying my head back on the pillow, I rubbed my fingers through Toya's hair while rotating my hips to follow the motion of her tongue. I moaned softly and tightened my grip on her hair when she inserted a finger then two and started pumping them inside and out my soaking wet pussy.

I started grinding on her fingers and mouth harder, not being able to suppress my moans, and I said, "Baby, I need to taste you."

While lifting her mouth but keeping her fingers in the same spot, she lifted her body up, scooted up in a crawl position, rotating her arm and fingers in my pussy. She turned her body so she could sit on my face in a sixty-nine position.

I scooted my body up just a little, so I could be in a mini sit-up-like position. I put my hands on her ass cheeks and opened them up. I kissed both cheeks before I put my tongue in her asshole. Toya's a freak, that's why I love sex with her so much. We're freaky together. As I'm going back and forth with my tongue from her pussy to her asshole, she's finger fucking me and stimulating my pearl tongue with her mouth, and with her grinding harder and harder, I felt like she's about to come. I pushed my thumb in her asshole while I went to attack her clit, and as soon as I sucked on it one good time, her legs started to shake, and as I'm slurping up her juices, I felt myself cum nice and hard at the same time.

We both lay there in the same potion, her pussy on my stomach with her head laid on the bed between my legs, with my pussy bumping her titties and my head lay back on the pillow, spent. After five minutes of just lying there, she changed positions and came to lay next to me, and I wrapped my arms around her to scoot her close.

She looked up and said, "You gonna spend the night with me?"

"Naw, ma, you know I can't do that, not tonight. And plus I have to be somewhere in the morning."

"Aight, that's cool You still coming over tomorrow so we can watch movies?"

I hated to disappoint her right now with her being so fragile, but the truth was I was just keeping close tabs on her because I'm tryna figure out who set me up to get robbed. The sex was good, shit, it was great, but that was just what it is. Toya was gettin' hopes that Imma leave Darnisha soon, but I'm not, I'm just irritated with her for the moment. I get like that at times. I guess I just spaced out because Toya cleared her throat asking, "So, are you?"

"Huh? What? Look, I gotta go. I'm already late, and I gotta early morning tomorrow. Hit me up around four o'clock. 'Kay?"

Sliding my arm up from under her and heading to the bathroom, I could hear her smacking and sighing under her breath. Shit, I could care less what the fuck I'm about to say to Darnisha's ass because it's about to be one hell of a night was all I could think of.

*****

Before turning the knob to my home, the only thing I could do was let out a deep breath before I went in the house. As I walked through the door, Darnisha was sitting right there on the couch in front of our plasma screen TV watching her favorite show *The L Word*, with a blanket on her lap. Before I could close and lock the door all the way, the remote control went flying past my head.

"On your way home, huh, Jay! It's one o'clock in the morning, and I called you at eleven when you was on your way home! Where were you! Huh? And don't lie!"

By then she was already in my face with all that finger pointed and neck moving. She got that shit bad. I swatted her hand and said in a deflated tone, "Babe, a second or two after I hung up with you, April called me asking if I wanted to stop by the after hour club she was at over on Central for a drink if I was out because she had to holla at me."

Looking at me straight in my eyes, she didn't know whether to believe me or not.

So I said, "Darnisha, babe, I needed a drink anyway because it's been a long day at the shop. I had to send Tony packing, I got into it with Anita again, and I needed to make sure my proposal was ready for Monday."

"What? Why did Tony have to leave the shop?"

I was happy that I was able to switch the topic from me to Tony and something other than where I was at tonight. "She been late on her booth fees for three months, and Anita did everything she possibly could to help her, but she's been late and not even paying the weekly payments. I just can't have that right now especially when next door is still sitting over there with a FOR RENT sign."

I own a duplex and only live in one while I rent the other out because I have no other use for it. My family lives in San Bernardino, and Anita never wanted it, so I put it on the market for rent. The inside was nice just like mine, upstairs, downstairs with three bed-rooms, three bathrooms, a living room, kitchen, and a back door to the patio out back. The only thing I hated was the fact that there's only a two-door garage and driveway. Other than that, it's home.

Walking upstairs and to our room, Darnisha followed me, "Aww, I feel bad for her. I really like Tony, maybe I'll give her a call on Monday."

Taking off my heels and throwing my blazer over our lounge seat we have in our room and walking toward the bathroom unbut-toning my slacks, I said," Darnisha, babe, I'm beat. I'm about to take me a quick shower to get that club smell off me, then Imma lay down because I have an early morning tomorrow."

She instantly rolled her eyes and gave me that what-you-just-say look before saying, "What the fuck, Janikka, you just got home." Raising her voice, she said, "Where the hell are you going so early in the morning?"

Stepping in the bathroom, I chose to ignore her and have her wait a minute before I answered.

I grabbed my toothbrush and toothpaste then turned on the water before I said, "It's Sunday, I got to go see Travis, and afterward we can go out to way or to your dad's. What you think?"

She didn't even answer me, she blew out a frustrated blow and walked out the room. What the fuck ever, I'm tired of her constant nagging anyways.

Stepping in the shower and feeling the hot water relaxed my body, and while I washed up, I let my mind drift off on trying to figure out how Imma tell my brother about what's going on, and what did he have important to tell me? Oh well, I'll know in a few hours. I turned off the water and stepped out the shower. I put on my pajama shorts and T-shirt, straightened up the bathroom, and walked in the room.

Seeing Darnisha already in bed, I turned off the light and slid in behind her. I pulled her close to me in a spooning position, kissing her ear, "I'm sorry, D. Imma be coming home early. I hate arguing with you, baby…I love you."

"I love you too, Janikka."

I kissed her again, hugged her closer to me, and fell asleep.

Chapter 17

Every time I walked inside this facility, I get the shudders. The visiting area was always clean, but the paint was chipped all along the wall. The chairs were the metal fold up kind that hurt my ass the entire time. The tables were small, it's no wonder as to how they had so many in this room with almost one hundred people at a time, and that's including inmates and visitors. I went to my little table in the corner of the room like I always do because Travis likes his privacy and to have his back up against the wall. I didn't get as many states today as I usually got when I am in this room.

I looked up at the clock just when Travis was escorted through the door and walked over to the table. I hugged him then said, "It was about time, I've been sitting here thirty minutes. What took so long?"

He smiled that one smile he always did when something good had gone his way.

"My bad, little sis. Did you see the lady officer who opened the door for me to come in?"

"Yeah, what about her?"

"Well, that's Johnson, the one I was telling you about."

Well, now I knew why the nigga was smiling and took so long. He probably got a quickie in somewhere, and looking at his face, I could tell that's just what happened.

"You're nasty. You kept me waiting so you could play when we got shit to handle today."

Changing his facial expression, he got serious real quick as he remembered that this wasn't just a call.

"Baby girl, I got a lot of shit to tell you, but first I gotta ask you, does the name Thornton ring any bells?"

Sitting back and hitting my back against the chair, I immediately sat back up and closed my eyes, trying to remember the name and place it somewhere, but I couldn't.

"Nah. I don't know that name, but what does it have to do with anything?"

"Okay, what about Micheal Thornton?"

And before he could finish the question, my eyes were as big as saucers as the name registered in my head. As if knowing that I just realized who it was, Travis said, "Yeah, the nigga you testified against three years back and Anita's boyfriend."

I was shaking my head. "No, but what does—"

I couldn't even finish my sentence before he started again, "Well, the nigga is the one that's been my celly for the last year."

My stomach dropped because I knew that the rest was about to be all bad as I listened to my brother talk.

"When he first became my celly, he was a transient, that mean he came from another prison which was Delano and got transferred here. I now know all this was planned but couldn't exactly pinpoint why. Then that's when I had Johnson get ahold of his visiting logons because he's been getting visits every Saturday since he's been here. And guess who his visitor is?"

Still shaking my head in disbelief, he didn't wait for me to answer like he knew that I was putting it together in my head.

"Right. Anita Jones, his baby mama, your best friend who also got on the stand. Now I didn't know about the court thing until I went hunting because I knew how he knew who I was. I just couldn't figure out what the beef was about, and it wasn't adding up until I saw a copy of his transcripts. Last Saturday, while he was on his visit, I went through his shit and whoops, up pops your name testimony against him on his spouse abuse and domestic violence case."

By now I was done putting everything together and found my voice. "So you're telling me all this shit against you, him getting at Cook skimming shit, probably getting info out of this bitch, all get back at me? But why?"

Then the answer to everything smacked me right in the face. "That bitch been setting me up and plotting on me the whole time, Travis!"

Disgusted with myself for allowing this to happen, I got up, asked Travis if he wanted something at the vending machine, and walked off toward them to collect myself. I couldn't break down in front of all these people, but right now I wanted to cry. Getting our drinks, I walked back to the table, handed him his Dr Pepper and sat down.

"So what happened to that drop three weeks ago?" Travis asked.

Then remembering the bad news, I had to share with him, and knowing that he was about to be upset, I just came out with it, "I was robbed."

"What!"

Just as I expected, Travis raised his voice a few octaves and got the CO's attention and had them looking over at us.

"Shh, shh, keep it down, the peoples are looking over here. Now listen, I'm fine, I just had a black eye and bruised rib."

"What the fuck you mean you're fine, you was robbed for God's sake, and of what?" Travis was mad, his nose was flaring and everything. "Who did it?"

"I'm not sure yet, but I got a few ideas because only a number of people know about my spot downtown, and that's where it happened. So I'm looking into some things, and when I handle things, then I'll let you know, but for now, I'm good."

Then he got serious. "Man, baby girl, shit is getting serious. I know it was fun while it lasted, but you gonna have to stop. Me and you both know you sitting on a pretty penny besides what was taken, so you need to think about shit."

Feeling my eyes tear up, I dabbed at them because I hated to see my brother so worried and scared for me. "I know B.I.G., and I'm done trust that. I just wanna get the muthafuckas who set me up, then Imma feel better and focus on opening up that retail store I was telling you about."

He smiled as if knowing I wanted to get off that topic and talk about something else. We talked about the new CO Johnson and how he was really feeling her then about me and my fucked-up situation between Toya and Darnisha.

Then he said, "Baby girl, you meant to tell me you back fucking with that crazy broad Tony?"

"Yeah, Toya. Not Tony, fucker, and the sex is great."

"Yeah, I could feel you on that because I'm really thinking about forgiving Cook because truth is she can suck the shit outta my joint, like no other had."

Laughing, we sat there and joked around for another hour or so before visiting was over. As I got up to hug my brother goodbye, he whispered in my ear and said, "The nigga is a dead issue, and Cook is next just like we planned."

I kissed his cheek and walked out of the visiting room knowing that Anita would be getting that call soon, if not already, and I'll be right there to comfort the sneak-ass bitch.

Instead of getting off the freeway on my exit, I kept going and headed toward the beach to clear my head. Sitting on this rock and throwing tiny pebbles into the water, I started trying to figure some things out. Whenever I needed to really sit and think, I always come to the beach. The water splashing against the rocks and seagulls chirping had always been soothing to me.

Damn! So the whole time I thought the bitch was my friend and while I was helping her out, she was watching me and setting me up. After Micheal went to jail, the bitch didn't have any money to put up or anything. I gave her a job; we started our side scandal together. I put her on, I helped her get where she's at today. I helped her move into that house she lives in, and all this was over for what? Because I helped her put away that nigga who was beating her senseless and cheating on her damn near every day? Heph. "I guess that's what friends are for," I said aloud.

I'm glad that Travis told me to stop meeting Cook because I would've been in jail if I would've made that last drop. Thinking of Travis, he's right, I need to stop with the client's shit. I make good money without the side hustle, but it was the double life part that I loved the most about it. Seeing that the person I was doing it with had been setting me up, I don't see why not stop. And stop renting

94

out that house downtown. Yeap, that's what Imma do. Imma tell Tashanda to give the owner a thirty-day notice and that I'll pay extra if the lease was now up. I'm kinda wondering now about that last robbery because Rick does his business alone, and he specifically told me that. I wouldn't be surprised if she had somebody there already waiting to get at me considering the nigga Micheal was actually turning state evidence against me to get jail free ticket with Anita's help. Now I see why the bitch be talking with so much venom.

I never thought twice about it until now even though I didn't know why I didn't see it before, I always felt something was up. I'm not trippin' though, I got a surprise for her ass. I'm not gonna crush her world just yet, but I am gonna get her. Right now, Imma be the friend she needed and thought that I still am when she get the news that her baby daddy is dead, and in time, all hell was about to break loose.

Looking down at my watch, it's going on seven o'clock. I rose up to leave, tossed the rest of my pebbles in the water, and as I'm walking toward my car, I put a smile on my face, satisfied with my plans that I have reserved for the bitch that claims to be my best friend.

In the car, I opened my phone and dialed Darnisha's number.

"Hello," she said.

"Hey, baby, be ready, I'm on my way."

"Okay."

And before she hung up, I hurriedly said, "Dress nice and elegant because I wanna dine somewhere really nice tonight as if we're celebrating." Then I hung up the phone.

On my drive to the house, I checked my voice mails and thought to myself that Imma have to let Toya go pretty soon because these messages were getting crazy and possessive.

Chapter 18

While I looked around the cemetery before the preacher started the burial sermon, I noticed a woman standing at the tree on the far side of the park. She had on a black dress with some overly big sunglasses that covered most of her face with a chic ponytail slicked to the back. She looked like she was watching me. I didn't pay it any mind and tuned back into what the priest was saying about Micheal's hard life and how gracious he was through it all. Tears were streaming down my face endlessly while I stared at my life inside that casket. I was holding onto li'l Micheal's hand tight, thinking that if I let it go, he was gonna leave me too. Li'l Micheal was fidgeting the whole time, not really understanding that the person we were burying was someone important. It's partially my fault because if he would've known that the man he saw in the casket in the black suit was his real father, then he would feel the pain I'm feeling.

When the prison warden called and told me about his death a few days ago, I was devastated. I didn't know what to do. I slept and got high until I couldn't feel myself think. Larnell asked me over and over again what was wrong, but I couldn't find my voice. All I could focus on was the fact that he was supposed to come home to me and li'l Micheal a couple weeks from the day he died. *What happened? What went wrong?* was all I could think. One day we were signing papers to testify against Janikka for his freedom, and now I'm burying him in the dirt. Looking up over at Janikka now put a bittersweet taste in my mouth because I promised to God I was gonna get her. Even if it killed me in the process because this was all her fault in every single way.

Then the preacher said, "From ashes to ashes, and dust to dust."

I wiped the back of my hand against more fallen tears, let go of li'l Micheal's hand, and placed the single white rose on top of the casket when it closed. Leaving my hand on the casket, I made Micheal a silent vow to get revenge on those who were responsible for his death. Stepping away from the casket, someone touched my arm. I turned to stare right into Janikka's eyes.

"Come on, let's go."

"You all go on ahead, Jay, I'll meet y'all back at the house, just give me a minute."

She reached out to hug me and rubbed my back. "I know it hurts, sweetie. Just know that I am here for you."

I hugged her back. "I know, Jay. I love you for always being there, now take little Micheal and I'll meet y'all in about an hour."

"Okay."

She turned to leave, grabbing li'l Micheal up in her arms. He was still so small to be five years old. He's gonna remind me so much of his father that it's gonna kill me. After I made arrangements for Micheal's burial, I asked Larnell if he wanted to go. Of course, he said no, which was what I expected from him anyways. Ever since that morning I pulled my gun out on him, he's been acting distant, which was fine with me because I've been trying to find a reason to get rid of him ever since I found out that Micheal was close to coming home. Now that he's never coming home, I don't know what to do. I used some of my share of what was in the office on the burial, but I have the jewelry and dope put away in storage. I split all the cash four ways between me, Larnell, Lamar, and his homie, the same on from the Rick robbery. That's another reason why Larnell had been distant and MIA because he'd been smoking up all that money with God knows who and tricking with whoever looks at him.

He was supposed to use the money to get himself up. It's been two weeks going on three since we got the money, but I yet to see it happen. I didn't notice the same woman that was standing next to that tree at the beginning of the burial had moved and was standing next to me until I saw her shadow and heard a leaf crunch. I looked up to see her looking at the casket. I wiped my eyes and cleared my throat then asked, "Do I know you?"

The woman looked up at me as if she was in a trance and then snapped out of it as if now being away of my presence.

"Umm, no, I'm sorry. I didn't mean to invade your privacy, I was just visiting a friend of mine and noticed your pain."

Not really interesting in conversing with a stranger at this time, I didn't comment. She didn't get the hint and said, "I'm sorry for your loss, the person must've been really close to you."

Turning to look at her and about to tell her to get lost, I looked at her face for the first time, and she looked vaguely familiar.

"Hey, don't I know you from somewhere? It look like I've seen you before."

As if she thought she wasn't hiding her face well enough, she reached up to push her glassed further onto her face.

She smiled. "I'm quite sure you don't know me." Then she turned to walk away.

At her receding back, I yelled, "Hey, what's your name?"

She turned back around and smiled then said, "Diamond."

Returning my focus back on the casket, I tried remembering where I heard that name before and tried to match it with the face. *Diamond. Diamond. Diamond.* I thought over and over again in my head and couldn't come up with anything. Seeing the cemetery people coming to close up the ground and to place a tombstone on this spot to mark his presence in life, I turned to walk toward my car. When I got inside the car and closed the door, I realized where I remembered seeing her at. It was at the House of Blues, talking to Toya at Darnisha's party. Not knowing that, that was important to know for Jay's sake, I pushed it out of my mind and started my drive to the house to meet up with Jay, Darnisha, and Larnell so we could go out to eat.

*****

Leaving Anita at the cemetery was a relief because I was irritated with just being around her sneak ass. When she called me about Micheal's death in the prison, I wasn't surprised. I was actually waiting on her call even though it took longer than I thought, it was right on time. I asked her if she needed any extra money or help arranging the burial ceremony, she said no to both, and I was happy about it. I was only trying to do the friendly thing in the awkward situation. I swore that I never knew people could be so treacherous. Anita actually looked me in the face on a daily basis like she wasn't planning on sending me to jail and taking my life away to save a nigga that does nothing but whoop her ass and cheat on her. But what did I expect when she settled for Larnell's broke ass? I guess love is truly blind. I wonder why he didn't go to funeral or burial service to support her, probably somewhere getting high. Pulling up in Anita's driveway, I saw that Larnell was home.

Looking over at Danisha, I asked, "Are you okay, baby?"

She looked at me and smiled "Yeah, I'm fine! It's just that Annita looked so sad back there. I've never seen her so sad before."

"Yeah, but Anita, she's strong. She's gonna be all right, beside she has me, you, li'l Micheal, and Larnell to call on if she needs help." Looking back at li'l Micheal, I said, "Well, not so much of li'l man back there, but she has us."

Laughing and reaching over to kiss me, she said, "You're right, I don't even know why I'm worried."

As we started getting out the car, I was thinking to myself, *I don't even know why you're worried either because you could've been as sad as her today if her and her boo plan would've been successful.* Except for I wouldn't have been in a casket but behind somebody's bars. Knocking on the door, Larnell said, "Hold on!"

When he finally opened the door, he was standing there sweating like he just ran a mile, and his eyes were as big as saucers. Yeah, I was thinking this nigga was high, walking in the living room, I knew he was high. You could smell the air freshener thick in the air, and that's why he was sweating, he was trying to straighten up and get the smell out the living room, but it didn't work. I looked over at Darnisha going to sit down, and she had her face scrunched up while li'l Micheal ran to his room.

I turned to Larnell and asked while my hand was over my nose, "What is that awful smell in here?"

Larnell was fidgeting with something on his shirt then walked over to the dining area to grab a chair then sat down and said, "What smell? What are you talking about, Jay?"

He said it with a kind of slur, but I recognized the voice. I caught it real clear, and to be sure, I wasn't tripping, and to hear the sound of his voice again with suspicion, I said, "Nigga, you know what it smell like. I can't describe it, like someone been burning paper."

As he was about to answer my question, the front door opened up with Anita walking in holding two big boxes of Church's Chicken saying "I wanted to go out but—" and stopped in midsentence when she reached the living room where you could automatically get a whiff of that ill smell. She looked at Larnell like she was going to kill him but tried to brush it off by walking in the kitchen. Looking at me while setting the food down and opening up the boxes, she said, "I'm not in the mood to be bothered with a lot of people around me. Where's Micheal?"

I pointed toward his room. She told for him to come out to eat then asked Larnell if he was hungry. When he opened his mouth to answer, my ears tuned up because I needed to know if I was hearing clearly.

He said, "Naw, I'm cool. Imma be in the back." Then he turned and looked at me. It seemed like he was about to say something but didn't. He shook his head, got up, and walked toward the back room.

Sitting in this living room, I felt my anger rising. I couldn't stay in this house one more minute after hearing Larnell's voice and now knowing that Anita was the one who set me up again to get robbed by her own boyfriend. That voice I heard before I blacked out was Larnell's, and now I'm sure of it slurred and all. My ears couldn't lie. When li'l Micheal ran out the room, I called him over to give me and Darnisha a hug. I raised up and told Anita that we were leaving.

She said, "What? Why? I just bought all this chicken."

"I forgot I got something to do, but I'll call and check on you later."

"All right, let me walk you to the door because I need to speak with you for a second."

Out on the porch after Darnisha gave Anita a hug, she walked off and got in the car. Anita turned to me.

"I know what you're thinking, but it's not bad."

This shit was crazy. She's actually standing in front of me telling me that Larnell smoking crack in the house was not that bad when I just realized she fucking set me up so a smoker could rob me.

Shaking my head, I asked, "How long has it been going on? And I hope it's not around my little man."

She shifted on her feet, something she did when she was getting ready to lie. "Not long, and, no, he doesn't do it while Micheal's in the house."

"Aye, Anita, you know what, that ain't my business, you feel me? But I will tell you this, you better be careful, that nigga got a habit, then all of a sudden you do too."

Anita shook her head. "It's not that, and I was gonna ask if I could get a week off so I could get myself together?"

I just looked at her, not surprised by the question and knowing that she was gonna probably use that time to get high and do whatever else she's plotting against me.

"That's cool. I'll have Tashanda hold the shop down and whatever else I may need, but besides all that, are you gonna be all right?" I asked.

"Yeah, I'm good."

She reached out to hug me then said" I love you so much" while rubbing my back.

"Me too," I said then walked off the porch, got in my car, and drove out of that area fast.

I didn't realize that I was really putting the pedal to the metal until Darnisha said, "Woah! Babe, slow the fuck down!"

I eased my foot off the gas and loosed up my death grip off the steering wheel.

She asked, "What's the matter?"

I looked at her like she was crazy. "What you mean? You smelled that shit just like I smelled it, and you saw how glazed that nigga's eyes were." That wasn't the real reason why I was upset, but she didn't need to know that.

"Yes, I smelled it, but what can we do about it? If Anita allows that, that's her boyfriend."

"That shit still don't make it acceptable. Li'l Micheal is there, and he getting high off that shit. Even in the house, which makes it worse."

"Well, I don't know what to say because I never knew Larnell got high off that shit even though I heard it before a while back, but I never saw it myself personally."

I didn't even respond because I was too engrossed in my thoughts to even pay attention to what Darnisha was saying. My focus was getting Darnisha home so I could go take care of some business.

Chapter 19

After Janikka left the house, I went inside, gave li'l Micheal a plate of chicken, macaroni and cheese, two biscuits and a slice of chocolate cake, and told him to go eat in his room. Once I made sure my li'l man was good and in his room, I walked in my room ready to chew Larnell, a new asshole for getting high in the living room again, knowing that Jay and Darnisha were coming over today.

When I walked in, he was sitting back on the bed with a pipe and crack on one plate and my nose candy on another plate as if he knew I wanted to get high but to also distract me from going off. I sat on the bed after closing the door and making sure it was locked so li'l Micheal won't just walk in. I grabbed my plate, made a couple of lines with my pinky, picked up my straw, and snorted the coke inside my nose. Then I tilted my head back so I could feel the drop down my throat because that's the best part.

After my drop, I looked Larnell and asked, "Why did you get high out there when I told you we were coming back here after the ceremony for Micheal?"

He humped his shoulder like it was no big deal. "Anita, I forgot about all that, and when the knock on the door is when I remembered."

"You would've remembered if yo ass wasn't getting high. I don't understand why you smoke that shit anyway. It fucking stinks!"

Larnell looked me in the eyes. "It may stink, but it gives you a high that makes you forget all your pain and troubles."

Then he put a piece of crack on the pipe and shoved it toward me so he could shut me up and not ruin his high. "Try it and tell me how you feel."

Letting my curiosity get the best of me, I reached for the pipe. "Here, nigga, give me the lighter so I can see why you feel the need to smoke this stinky shit every day."

Before I put the fire on up against the pipe, I heard Larnell say, "Yeah, we'll see how you'll be feeling after you hit that shit."

If I would've looked at him while he was talking, I would've seen the malice in his eyes and mischievous smirk on his face, but instead, I had my eyes fixated on the task at hand. I put the pipe in my mouth and flame on the rock and watched it melt while I sucked in all the smoke down my lungs. I took one long pull then I handed it back to Larnell. As soon as I was about to say I don't feel anything, my ears started ringing, and I felt my whole body relax. My pussy started tingling, and it felt like I just had an orgasm right there in my panties.

I put my hand in my pants to feel myself so wet and moist between my legs, like I hadn't had sex in ages. I sat there feeling like the whole world just lifted off my shoulders, and before I realized what I was doing, I stuck my arm out toward Larnell to reach for the pipe again because I wanted another hit if I was gonna be feeling like this.

Larnell happily and hurriedly handed the pipe over and started taking off my pants while I was pulling one again on the pipe. When he slipped off my panties and I felt his tongue on my hot spot, I immediately started cumming. I don't know what type of feeling I'm having, but whatever it was, I loved it. I circled my hands on his head, humping his face and pushing it hard against my pussy, begging him to go deeper.

I removed one hand and started playing with my titties, sucking on my own nipple, feeling like Larnell's hands on me only weren't enough. I was horny beyond control. I squirmed underneath Larnell and asked him to put it in. He happily obliged and pushed deep inside me, pumping in and out hard. I didn't know if it was the shit I just smoked, but it seemed like my hearing had intensified because all I could hear was his sex slapping up against my sex so loud in my ear it was turning me on.

I moaned loud and grabbed onto his ass while I wrapped my legs around his waist, trying to push him deep, deep inside of me. I lifted up and bit down on his shoulder; he then turned me over on my stomach, roughly snatching me back so he was again inside of me. I put my hand on the headboard and had the other on my slit, rubbing it fiercely while he was smacking my ass hard and pulling my hair. Six more minutes of that rough sex, then me and Larnell both came long and hard at the same time then collapsed.

Laying there spinning, Larnell reached for his pipe and took another long pull then stuck his arm out to hand it to me. I looked at my plate then back at the pipe, and I grabbed the pipe and took me another pull, thinking to myself, *This ain't nothing, just this one time.* Boy, was I wrong! I just picked up a habit that would be hard to kick.

I turned to see Larnell rubbing on his dick, and I was more than ready to hop on it.

*****

Pulling up at the shop today, I knew I had a lot to get done in a short amount of time because I had plans to meet Darnisha for lunch. A couple of days ago, I told Anita that she could have a week off that she asked for, but I'd been trying to call her to see how she was holding up since the funeral but been only getting her voice mail. Which was cool either way because after I got that confirmation that Larnell was the one who robbed me, I couldn't do anything but set up my next move for Anita. Anita didn't know that I knew everything that she had originally planned for me and that she had been setting me up the entire time, but she was about to feel my wrath sooner than she probably realized.

Getting out of my car and walking in my shop, I couldn't help putting a smile on my face from the warm welcoming feeling I always felt when I walked inside. My place of business into the gossip and love every day. For some odd reason with my mind being everywhere else, I still acknowledged the fact that my new stylist, Miya, was looking hella sexy in a mini jean skirt, a DKNY red T-shirt that fit perfectly around her breast and flat stomach, and some red open toe strappy heels that complemented her pedicured toes. *Damn,* I thought to myself, *she sure is beautiful.*

Right when I was about to walk past her and into the back, she reached out to grab my arm. I stopped and asked, "Wassup?"

"Hey, Jay. I was wondering when you get a minute later on today if I could come speak with you?"

Trying to keep my eyes on her face and not on her long legs or breast, I said "Sure" and kept toward the back. I had too many things to do, and flirting wasn't one of them, so I had to focus on the task at hand.

I spoke to Tash and to make sure that Damonte was still coming in to see me today because I had some business for him. Once I got into my office, I had to call Cook because she had been blowing up my cell phone. I'd been avoiding her because I already knew that this had everything to do with the sexual harassment suit my brother had filed against her. Travis was a cold nigga for that though, I didn't know he was gonna go that doop with the bitch, but that's what you get when you betray a muthafucka that was nothing but good to you.

She was lucky that she's only getting that because if it was left up to me, she'd be kicking up dirt like that nigga Micheal and soon to be Larnell. When working as a CO for the state penitentiary, a sexual harassment suit charged against you can cause you to lose not only your job but leave a reputation that will lead to permanent unemployment.

Sitting down at my desk, I picked up the phone, dialed her number, and allowed the phone to ring. Once Cook picked up the phone, she immediately started crying.

I said, "Wassup, you called me last night?"

Her voice was muffled, and she was sniffling. So I said, "Hole up, wait, wait, I can't understand a word you're trying to say."

"Sorry! I just don't understand why he's doing this to me."

"What are you talking about, Cook, and who's doing what to you?" I asked.

"You already know what Travis is up to, Janikka, don't play me like that."

Now this hoe had got her nerves. She's done already playing herself. The bitch was lucky that I couldn't call the consequences, but for right now, Imma be cool.

"Listen, Cook, I'm sorry for whatever it is you're going through, but right now, I'm busy and can't really talk. So you try to have a good day."

I hung up the phone before she could say anything else smart or out the side of her mouth. I leaned back in my chair, allowing my mind to wander about everything that I've been going through these past weeks. Darnisha had been complaining about feeling neglected, but for real, I couldn't blame her because I'd been around her physically, but my mind had been everywhere else. When Cook called my phone last night, I was in the middle of giving her the attention that she needed. Last night was good, so I made plans with her to have a late lunch. I started thinking about why I hadn't heard from Anita when a knock at the door interrupted my thoughts.

Snapping out of my trance, I told, "Come in!"

Damonte poked his head inside and asked if it was a good time.

"Yeah, come on in. I was waiting on you and just asked Tashanda if you were still coming by. Wassup, man?"

I got up, reached my hand out to slap his hand into mine, and clasped my other hand over both of his.

"Have a seat, man, how you doing?"

"I'm good. You know, just tryin' to stay out the way, and you know I wanna thank you for helping me out."

"Aww, come on. You're like family. Shit, you are family. Don't even worry about that, but I gotta be straight with you. I didn't call you over here to talk about how you been doing."

He leaned back in the chair. "Aight, wassup then?"

"Okay, listen to me. What I'm about to tell you is to stay right here in this room. I don't even want you telling Tashan about this, agreed?"

"Yeah, you got my word."

I looked him in the eyes and believed that it would stay in this room. I started telling him everything about the robbery that happened to me about a month ago, to my own so-called best friend,

Anita, being the one who set the whole thing up, and having her nigga, Larnell, do the dirty work. By the time I qas finished talking, he was leaned up and shaking his head in awe, I assumed, or shaking it like what the fuck.

He said, "Damn, girl, I didn't know you was into all that type of shit. But for real, ya girl is scandalous. I would have never guessed that. She seemed to be so cool, trustworthy, and down the earth. But no offense, you still haven't told me why you called me here."

I started smiling. "Well, actually, I was getting to that. I need you to handle the nigga, Larnell, for me, and I know he be over there in your neighborhood getting his dope."

Damonte was known as an enforcer and lightweight hustler from 97 Gangsta Crips. His main block was ninety-seventh and Budlong on the west side of LA.

"You've probably seen him but didn't recognize him because he try to stay incognito. That's why he go way yonder to yo side of town in the first place."

Damonte leaned back in the chair, looking like his wheels were turning inside of his head. I leaned back also and let the quietness take over the room.

"So what exactly do you have in mind for the nigga, or do you want me to do whatever it is I choose to do?"

I looked up at him and slid him a piece of paper that was already on my desk with Anita's home address and every other important information he may need to get at Larnell.

"I want you to do whatever it is you need to do to make the nigga disappear without much noise and attention. I mean the nigga is a real crackhead too, so it should be smooth."

He nodded his head. "And besides that, I'm ready to break bread with you, tell me what it is you want."

He laughed. "Naw, Jay, it's cool, consider it payment for what you did for me, not even including that I'm more than happy to help you get back at Anita. You just be careful and stop trusting these untrustworthy-ass bitches.

"Yeah. All right, trust me that's what I'm gonna do. I appreciate this, Damonte, real talk."

"Don't trip, it's all love. Well, let me get up out of here, I got somewhere I gotta be."

"All right, thanks again. I'll holla at you."

Damonte got up to leave, and I put my head back on my chair once the door was closed. Thinking to myself, *This is gonna be a long day.*

Chapter 20

Lying here next to Larnell, I didn't know how long I'd been in the room. I just started hearing banging on the door, that's what made me lift up. I shoved Larnell.

"Get up, get up. Somebody banging on the front door."

Larnell made a grumbling sound. "Ain't nobody at the door, you trippin', Anita."

I shoved him again. "I ain't trippin', this is fourth time I've heard fucking banging, and every time, you told me I'm trippin'. Just get you lazy ass up and go check."

He mumbled something under his breath then got up, yanked his pants on, and started toward the door. When he opened the room door, Micheal ran in the room yelling "Mommy! Mommy!" with ashen cheeks like he'd been crying. He jumped on the bed and into my arms and hugged me real tight like he hadn't seen me in days, which was weird, I just gave him some dinner then sent him to his room. I pulled him back and sat him at the foot of the bed.

Then I asked, "Boy, what you been crying for?"

"I was crying because I was hungry and made a mess. I tried to come get you, but you never came out."

I pulled my head back, trying to figure out why he was even hungry, then I remembered the banging and Larnell telling me that it's nothing. I remembered just sitting on this bed hitting the pipe with crack on it that Larnell just kept handing me. I remembered Larnell kept saying, "Where ya going? He's all right. Here, hit this."

We did line after line, hit after hit, and fucked like it was no tomorrow. I never once realized that it'd been daylight two days in a row before right now. I reached out and hugged Micheal so tight and said, "I'm so sorry, honey. Mommy was asleep."

And in his childlike voice, he said, "Mommy, you been sleep a long time because I haven't been to school or nothing. I just slept in front of your door."

I grabbed him again close and vowing to myself not to hit that shit again. It made me incoherent and forget everything around me. I pushed li'l Micheal back and told him to wait for me in the kitchen. As I was walking in the hallway, I was about to walk by Larnell when he said, "Told you, you was trippin'. Nobody at the door."

I looked at him like he was fucking crazy. "What you mean nobody was at the door. Are you stupid? My fucking son is hungry and been banging on the room door for two days while you had me in there holed up, shoving that damn pipe of your in my mouth and fucking me in every which way."

I pushed him aside and kept on toward the kitchen to feed my baby. I had to be honest with myself that I knew I wasn't trying to feel. I didn't want to be here anymore; it just saddened my heart that I put my child in a position in which I had no control. I couldn't believe myself and how that high took me somewhere else. Like it captivated my whole body and mind with just one hit. Damn. Fixing a sandwich real quick so Micheal could eat something right then and there, I started pulling out a skillet to fry some sausages and bacon then pulled out another skillet for the pancakes.

Once I had that going, I started cleaning up Micheal's mess in his attempt to make something to eat.

"So what exactly did you eat love while Mommy was asleep?" I asked, hoping he ate at least a slice of bread or orange something.

He looked up from his sandwich with the most beautiful dark brown eyes, looking like a mini version of the wonderful man I just buried two days ago. It seemed like it was yesterday when I saw Micheal coming out of the gas station on Imperial and Western right as I was going in. I bumped right into him on accident and made him drop his slush and swisher sweets. I offered to buy it for him again if he came back inside to get the stuff. But he declined and walked back inside the gas station.

After I purchased my stuff and paid for my gas, I walked back to my car my dad just bought me for graduation. While I was pumping my gas, Micheal came over and said, "So how do you plan to pay me back for your little stumble earlier, Ms.?"

I looked up and into the prettiest deep brown eyes I ever saw. He was 6'3" with an all-muscular frame like he's been locked up before, with soft, baby smooth, light brown skin, a wavy fade, rocking some all-white Air Force One's looking like they were fresh out the box. With some Enyce jeans on to match the white Enyce collared T-shirt he had on, he had a diamond stud in his ear with a watch that was just as fly. The nigga was fly himself, and I was at a loss for words as I Just stood there looking into them deep brown eyes of his.

Then I cleared my throat and said, "Well, I offered to buy it for you, but you said no. So what do you want me to do? I said I was sorry."

He looked at me. And when he did, my heart skipped a beat, and I felt like he was looking into my soul.

"So how about this then, let's go out to a movie or something?"

I don't know what made me agree, knowing that I didn't know him, and my dad would have a fire if I started dating some thug as he said. But I agreed, and we grew to love and trust each other as we created a bond nobody understood.

Even in death, Micheal will always have my heart. And looking at Micheal Jr. sitting at the table eating that sandwich made my heart ache. *God, please, forgive me for neglecting my baby. I will never do it again.* Unbeknownst to me, that was a promise I couldn't keep.

"Did you hear me, Mommy?" I heard Micheal say and snapped away from my memories.

"Naw, baby. I'm sorry, what did you say?"

"I said I ate some bologna and bread until you came out of your room later. But you never came out, so I did it until you came out right now."

Shaking my head and turning my attention back to the stove, I said over my shoulder, "Well, my baby, you not gonna have to worry about that again because Mommy not gonna sleep for a long time no more. Now after you finish your sandwich, go in there and get ready for school."

After Micheal ran to his room to get dressed, I finished up the pancakes, turned off the stove, and went to go to take a quick wash up, put on some sweat and a T-shit so I could drop him off and come back home to clean up. When I walked back in the dining area after putting on my clothes, Micheal was already seated at the table eating and talking to Larnell. I told li'l Micheal to hurry and meet me in the car when he was done. I was irritated and needed to smoke a blunt really quick.

So I stepped out on the porch, sat down, and blazed up before Micheal came running out. Twenty minutes later, me and Micheal was on the road on our way to his day care.

"Mommy, you stinky." Micheal said.

"Boy, shut up. Mommy don't stinky, you stinky."

He started laughing. "Nuh-uh. Mommy, I got in the tub while you were sleeping. Imma big boy." He was smiling really big at himself.

I pulled up at the school and walked in to sign him in for the day. I didn't notice people raising their eyebrows when I walked by until the lady at the desk said, "Ms. Jones, I need to know the reason why Micheal hasn't been to school in a couple of days?"

"Well, his father just died, so excuse me for not calling you first before I found out I had to bury the love of my life!"

I signed my baby in, looked at her like she was crazy, and was about to cuss her out but thought better of it. And I just said, "Thank you, and I'll see you later on."

The bitch was still talking, trying to apologize while I walked away.

*****

Before I could make a call to Anita, my cell phone started ringing. I picked it up to hear an automated operator telling me that I had a collect call from a California institution. After I pressed 5, I said, "Wassup, big bro, you sound chippery today, what's going on?"

"Shit, nothing, just wanted to hear your voice. I haven't heard from you in a minute. So how is everything out there?"

I knew that he was referring to the situation with Micheal and Cook.

"Aww, not too much of nothing. I attended a burial service two days ago, and today I got an awkward phone call from ole girl that's been bothering you up there."

We both started laughing and just started shooting the shit about me coming up there Sunday until our time ran out. Right before the phone call ended, there was a soft knock on my office door. "Come in!" I yelled.

Miya came strutting in like she was on a runway looking at me, smiling and licking her lips. Man, I swear in this moment I could kiss them pretty-looking lips, but I kept it professional just in case she wasn't on my side of the track.

"Wassup, Miya, right? What can I do for you?"

The look in her eyes let me know what was really up.

"Well, Jay. That's really what I came back here to find out."

That didn't take me by surprise, but I was still skeptical, and for real I needed to relieve some frustration, and what better way to do that than to dig in some pussy.

"Close the door, sweetheart, and make sure it's locked."

I couldn't help myself, the scent of new pussy kept me from resisting temptation. She walked back to me behind my desk and straddled my lap. I put my hands in her hair and pulled her face toward mine. Her lips were as soft as they looked. She snaked her tongue in and out of my mouth while I rubbed my fingers up and down her thighs under her skirt. In my head, I knew that I didn't' have a lot of time because I had to meet with Darnisha soon.

I leaned back and looked in her eyes to see nothing but lust, and I was so ready to feel her wetness. I pulled her up from my lap and sat her on my desk, lifting her skirt up to her waist. Through the lace thong, I could see that her pussy was freshly shaved. I licked my lips and started kissing her again. Trailing my kisses toward her neck, I slid my fingers through the side of her thong to feel her heat and wetness. Damn, I had to lean my head back because that pussy was wet as fuck.

I had to ask, "What I do to deserve something like this?"

She looked at me and said, "Every time I see you, my pussy is like this. Since day one."

She put her hands on my face and pulled me back to her mouth. My head was in a frenzy, but my fingers were skillfully caressing her pearl tongue, rubbing around her entryway while sliding one finger in and out of her pussy. She was grinding on my fingers, and her pussy was getting wetter and wetter. My other hand started pulling up her T-shirt so I could get one of her titties in my mouth. Once her nipples popped out, it was so brown and round; her areola looked like it needed my mouth around it. I quickly wrapped my mouth around that nipple. Damn, this pussy was so wet it got me wanted to taste it.

I slid my fingers out and put them into my mouth. *Hmm*, I moaned from the taste of her on my fingers. I quickly put them back inside of her warm walls. My kisses started to trail to her stomach. As I was about to kneel in front of her, my cell phone started ringing. Damn. I put my finger to my mouth to shush Miya because I knew it was Darnisha.

Grabbing my cell phone, I said, "Hello?"

"Babe, I'm outside. You ready?"

I took my fingers out of Miya and straightened myself out.

"Yeah, love, I'm coming out right now. Just wait for me in the car. You're driving."

Looking at Miya pulling down her skirt made me wanna make other lunch arrangements.

"Okay, hurry up!"

After hanging up the phone, I started kissing Miya again. It was something about this girl that I wanted to get to know. "Listen, Miya, we gonna definitely have to finish this. Make sure you don't have nothing to do tonight. I wanna see you for sure!"

"You got that, and hopefully we won't be interrupted."

She kissed me again and walked out the door. I washed my hands in the bathroom, locked up my office, and headed out. When I got in the car, Darnisha asked me why I was smiling so hard.

I kissed her cheek and said "I got a lot done so far, but I got a lot more work to do, and I'm happy I get a little break with you before tonight comes." with all thoughts of Miya spreading wide open in my mind.

Chapter 21

Today I was planning on going to the shop, but for some reason, I still wasn't feeling it. I called Jay and told her that I needed a few more days. We've talked a time or two since the burial, and I think it was more of a relief than a struggle to deal with. For some strange reason, the lady that was at the cemetery kept popping in and out of my mind. I felt lost and all disheveled.

I hadn't hit the pipe with Larnell, but I couldn't lie, I really wanted to. I'd been busy showering li'l Micheal with all my attention. The school cleared up his two-day absences after I had a little talk with the principal about their little receptionist, and it's a new receptionist at the front desk. I could honestly say though that I do miss the shop and the laughs that came from being there.

Getting ready to walk back inside of the house, I knew that I was just going to do the same thing I'd been doing every day after I dropped off Micheal at school. Which was nothing but cry, powder my nose, and pretend to have myself together. When really all I wanted to do was to escape, escape the heartache and emptiness that I felt inside.

These feelings made me hate Janikka so much more. I wanted to kill this bitch. I wanted to take away everything and everyone that she loves. She didn't deserve happiness in no type of way. I'm starting to feel like I hated myself. I had no reason to yearn, want, or live anymore. Micheal was my definition of true love, if I ever knew one. And I fucked up, I'm the reason why he's not here with me today.

No! It's that bitch Jay's fault. If she would've just minded her own damn business and stayed the fuck out of mine. Fuck this shit! I wanna go back to that place Larnell took me to. I don't wanna fight these urges anymore.

Walking inside the house, I screamed out, "Larnell! Larnell!"

"What, Anita! Why the fuck are you screaming!"

"Nigga, I wanna get high. Take me there, please."

Damn, I couldn't believe I was begging for the shit that I couldn't stand. But at this point, I just didn't give a fuck. The nigga I'm with obviously didn't give a fuck because he doesn't have a problem sticking that glass pipe in my mouth.

"Anita, is that all because there was no reason for you to be screaming if that's all you wanted. Come on, woman! Let's go in the room, but I'm telling you now, we gonna need some more because I ain't got much right now."

"All right, what you gonna need? Or do you wanna just go get it right now so we don't have to stop once we get started?"

This nigga actually started laughing at me and shook his head.

"Damn, Nita, yeah, come on. We can go pick some up, but I'm driving and you're staying in the car."

"Okay, let's go, and remind me that I gotta call Jay so she can pick up li'l Micheal for me."

*****

After getting off the phone with Anita, I felt like something was off with her. I gave her more days than she asked for because I wanted her to stay away from me for real anyways. Everything had been going cool. Me and Darnisha were back straight, she wasn't feeling neglected no more. I've been seeing Miya on a regular now; I am getting to know this girl, and I am loving it. Everybody in the shop knew that we had a thing going on because she couldn't keep her eyes in her head or her hands off me. You knew that extra friendly shit.

I wasn't tripping though because I had Toya at a distance and Darnisha happy. When I went to go see Travis last weekend, everything with Cook was just about closing out. The suit was filed, and now ISW had her on paid leave while they were investigating the case. I could honestly say that life was getting better from all the havoc that was just going on around me just weeks earlier. Having patience was what was working for me because I knew in time that everything would be going great.

Chilling in my office with Miya, I didn't expect to be interrupted by a knock at the door. I told Miya to stand up from sitting on my desk because I knew Darnisha was at work, but just in case it was her, I didn't need any drama.

"Come in."

Toya walked in my office like she owned the place and straight over to me then kissed my lips. Miya smacked her lips, rolled her eyes, and put her hands on her hips. Toya looked up at Miya and looked her up and down. "Excuse me, but do we have an issue?" she asked Miya.

Miya looked at me. I said, "Miya, would you excuse us, please? Imma finish talking to you right after I handle this."

Toya looked at me with a smirk on her face then said, "Ohh, I see what's going on here. Is this your new shop plaything?" Then she looked at Miya again. "Don't worry, baby, you're not the first and you won't be the last. So, yes! Excuse us."

Miya looked like she wanted to say something but just decided to walk out and slammed the door while she was at it.

I immediately pushed Toya back from out of my face. "What the fuck, ma! Don't just be coming in here doing shit and saying shit like that!"

"Oh, what, you didn't like that? Well, next time, you shouldn't let the entire shop know what you're doing!"

"What! Girl, me and Miya is just friends."

"Right, and me and Diamond was just hanging out. You know what, Jay, fuck you! Every time I feel like we could be getting somewhere, you always do something to let me know that ain't the case!"

"Toya, I never told you anything different than what you already knew. We were just messing around because I missed you as much as you missed me."

Toya started shaking her head. "You know what? You're a selfish son of a bitch, and sooner or later, you're going to find yourself alone because you fuck over everyone and everything that's been good to you!"

And on that note, with tears going down her face, she stormed out of my office and out of the shop. Looking outside of my office door, I screamed "What is everybody looking at! Get back to work!" then I closed my door.

Before I could sit down, my cell phone started ringing. It was li'l Micheal's school. I hurried up and answered the phone.

"Hello? Yes, I'll be there right away. Thank you."

I grabbed my jacket and told Tashanda to lock up tonight and rushed out of the shop.

Chapter 22

Larnell hadn't come back yet, and it'd been a whole day. We ran out of dope last night, and I couldn't get up to go with him, so he went on his own saying that he was gonna be right back.

It'd been a crazy couple of weeks. Janikka had been keeping li'l Micheal for me until I get myself together. Well, it ain't like I had too much to say about it after the school called her to pick up li'l Micheal when I forgot. Well, I didn't forget, Larnell didn't remind me to call her, so I thought I had already asked her to pick him up. So when she came barging in here and caught the pipe dead in my mouth, I couldn't say shit or deny anything.

I was caught up in my own cloud of smoke literally. She screamed at me, went in li'l Micheal's room and packed his clothes up. She'll come by once a week to tell me li'l Micheal misses me and wanted to see me, but what could I do? I was a mess. I was fucked up in the head, and I was telling myself that this will only be momentary and that I will snap back. Who the fuck was I kidding? My only focus was that pipe, and right now, I needed a fucking hit.

Where the fuck is Larnell? I'm tired of waiting. So I got in the car and drove to the spot that Larnell took us to all the time. I didn't know exactly what house he went to, I just knew that he walked in this alley. Walking deeper in the alley, I saw a few people standing in like a hideaway spot and tried my luck.

"Hey, wassup. Can I get something?
One of the dudes said, "Who are you?"
"I'm Nita, Larnell's old lady."
"You talking about Celly Nelly?"
"Yeah. Larnell."

The dude looked me up and down then took me to the back. "What you want?"

"Well, I got $200, so lono."

"Aight, here, Imma hook you up."

Back out in the alley and on my way to the street, I saw a man lying face down. I was compelled to keep walking until I noticed the tennis shoes on his feet. I ran over to him knowing that that was Larnell. Tears already streaming down my face, I rolled him over, and oh my god, it was Larnell all beaten up and bruised, not breathing.

"Oh my god!" I screamed. "Somebody help me!"

No one came to help, and no one listened to my cries. Where the hell was I? I held him a second longer, but the hit I needed was calling me more than the fact that I needed to get help for Larnell. Larnell was lying in that alley dead, and I had to leave him there. I got inside and numbed myself to where I couldn't feel myself to think about Larnell's body in that alley ever again.

In this moment, I was lost, and I now knew that I'm no longer in control of this drug but the drug is in control of me.

*****

Last night, I didn't expect a call from Damonte, but I got one letting me know that everything was everything. I didn't expect to hear from Anita, but I'd see her next week sometime.

"Here I come, honey!"

Walking into the living room, I knew that today was gonna be a good day. Darnisha and li'l Micheal were already dressed and ready to go to school and work.

"Baby, are you picking up li'l man or am I?" Darnisha walked over to me and kissed me on my cheek while whispering in my ear that I look nice.

"Thank you. Umm, I'll pick him up because I'm leaving the shop early today. I have something planned for the three of us tonight."

"Oh, okay!"

I turned to li'l Micheal. "And how you doing this morning?"

"I'm good, Auntie, are we gonna go see Mommy tonight?"

It's so sad, but he asked me this every day. "No, baby. Not tonight. I told you, Mommy is on a vacation, and when she comes back, we'll go see her. She's not herself, okay, little man?"

"Okay, Auntie Jay. I'm ready for school."

This whole thing broke my heart, but it'll be better soon. He just needs a little time, he'll come around.

Chapter 23

Three months later

Sitting outside of Anita's house, I knew that I had to hurry up with this conclusion because Miya had told me already that she had a special evening planned for us at the Hilton, so I was tryna get there. We've been going strong; she was officially my side chick. Even after the incident at the shop with Toya, it didn't deter us from fucking with one another. Yeah, she had an attitude, but when I explained to her that Toya was in the wrong, we've been better than ever.

Damonte came and knocked on my window and let me know that everything was ready. Well, today was the day. Walking into the garage, I couldn't help but to put my hand over my mouth from the strong pungent smell of gasoline. I knew that Anita didn't see this coming. I just left her house. I pretended to leave so I could leave the front door unlocked to easily let Damonte and his partner in the house. Anita was now a bona fide crackhead. Li'l Micheal had been with me and Darnisha ever since that phone call from the school.

I refused to subject my li'l man to the bullshit that Anita had put herself into, and every week I went to check on her, it seemed to get worse and worse. It went from her no cleaning up the house to her not washing her ass to her not eating or giving a fuck about anything. As I stood here and looked at her drenched in gasoline, crying and trembling, I don't understand how we ended up in this spot. But as I drew in a breath, I let the little soft spot I had left for her die in that moment. I slowly started walking toward her.

While looking at her sweat, everything that she put me through was flashing in my mind, which instantly made me angry, and I slapped the shit out of her then snatched the blindfold off her face, giving her a chance to adjust her eyes.

"So, you grimy bitch. I bet you didn't know I knew it was you who set me up and tried to ruin me this whole entire time. You can stop with all them muthafucking tears though! Answer me this. Why? What reason do you have to do this to me? Oh, wait! I can answer my own question, was it for Micheal? Yeah, it was! Hmph. All this, our friendship, your son being motherless, Larnell and Micheal kick up dirt. For what? Love!"

Laughing, I couldn't believe it. This bitch was just sitting here with her head hanging low not saying shit, it's just making me madder! So I slapped her again.

"Anita, I should've known you were stupid and a simple bitch when you was letting a nigga beat on you but even more when you allowed a crackhead to live under your room with you and your son!"

"Fuck you, Jay!" she screamed and then had the audacity to spit on me.

"Hmph. Fuck me, huh? Yeah… Well, it seems to me you're the only one that's to be fucked. Before I send you to hell, Imma give you a hell here on earth!"

I put the gag back in her mouth and watched her eyes get bucked as I pulled the matches out of my pocket and struck one. "Best wishes, bitch, there ain't no bitch that could be mickey with me and live to talk about it."

I threw the match on her and watched her set on fire for a second then walked out of that garage without an ounce of regret.

*****

Pulling up at the Hilton, I called Miya and let her know that I was on my way up. When I was at the house with Darnisha and li'l Micheal, I got the text from Miya with the room number and letting me know that she was ready and waiting on me. I honestly couldn't wait because after the day I had, I was ready to relax and get freaky. I didn't think Miya was about this life, but, boy, was I wrong. Miya's young ass was a freak and a sex addict I could get used to.

We've been trying all types of new different shit in the bedroom, so I was more than curious to see what she had planned for us tonight. When I walked in the room, the lights were dim, candles were glowing out on the bed from handcuffs, dildos, body edibles to chocolate syrup, cherries, and whipped cream. But when Miya came out of the bathroom with another woman with a body just as flawless as hers behind masks and sexy lingerie on, I couldn't stop the smile that spread across my face.

"Well, this is a lovely surprise."

Miya walked up on me and pressed her lips against mine, pulling back and shushing me with her finger. The other woman got on the bed and cat crawled to the center of the bed. Miya turned my head so I could face the woman on the bed while she spread her legs wide open and placed one hand on her pussy and another in her mouth. She started opening her legs then closing them back while she was rubbing her hands all over her body.

She looked at Miya and signaled her to come over to her with her finger. I stood there watching in pure lust, ready for the night's events. Miya crawled on the bed to her and straddled her lap. They started kissing and started grinding their hips together. Once their lips unlocked, they called for me to join them. I kissed the other woman while Miya started taking off my shoes and clothes. The woman reached under my shirt and lifted it over my head while never letting up on the rhythm they had me on.

My eyes were already rolling in the back of my head. If I wasn't in such a lusty state, I would've been paying attention to this mystery woman's face, but that wasn't important to me at the moment. I tried taking off Miya's lingerie, but she pushed my hands aside and said, "Wait. Baby, this show is for you. Now slide on back."

The woman handed Miya the handcuffs, and I was told to put my arms back to the headrest. I obliged, loving the fact that I was gonna be submissive to two beautiful women...but once both of my hands were cuffed and they started laughing, I instantly became confused then angry.

"Miya, wassup?"

"Wassup? Oh, Jay, wanna know wassup, babe?"

"Babe? What the fuck is going on?"

As the woman pulled off her mask, I looked at her face and tried to remember where I knew her from. Then she started talking.

"Ain't no need to try to remember who I am. I'm Diamond, Micheal's little sister. Yeah, and Miya here, this is my woman and soul mate of six years. And this here, oh, this is where it ends for you. Micheal wanted me here in California to take care of you, and Imma avenge my brother's death tonight!"

My head was literally spinning. My mind was everywhere. I couldn't believe this punk-ass bullshit. I've been getting mickied the whole time.

"How could you do this, Miya? I can't believe—" and before I could finish, somebody started banging on the door.

To be continued.

Acknowledgments

I want to first thank God for continuing to give me the strength and courage to keep going no matter what. Without his abundance of love and grace upon me, I can't say for certain where I will be because I am truly blessed. I also want to thank my family and close friends, Roneese, Travis, Keevie, Danielle, Tyrisha, Keyshay, Caprice, Tyrone, Kevon, Toneyay, Alexis, Maurice, Latoya (my Lily Flower), and there are so many more that I can add to the list, but I want to thank you all for always believing in me and giving me the support needed during difficult times. My mother, Carolyn Welch, I want to thank you for teaching me survival skills and instincts at such a young age; as a single mother of five children, you did an amazing job.

I also want to thank the rough-around-the-edges teenage girl that I was back in the day because she gave me the opportunity to grow into the woman that I am today. I have grown so much from the girl that used to love to be in trouble and an adrenaline junkie fanatic. I've matured from the young lady that stepped into CCWF at the age of eighteen and returning back into society at the age of twenty-five. I am now twenty-eight years old and sees nothing but the best in my future. I also want to take the time out to thank my readers, if you are now holding this book in your hand, thank you for giving me the opportunity to take you into a world of creation.

About the Author

Drucilla was born and raised in Long Beach, California, but she now resided in Moreno Valley. She is very family oriented and enjoys spending her free time with family and close friends. Drucilla is free-spirited, kindhearted, optimistic, trusting, loyal, and believes in uplifting all those around her. Drucilla started writing while confined in a small two-man cell in the Central California Women's Facility in Chowchilla, California, on the back pages of the *Title 115* handbook.

During this time, Drucilla felt that she was in a very low point in her life and found an escape through writing, not allowing her mind to be imprisoned like her body. Drucilla stayed true to herself, found her worth, and accomplished several great things while being incarcerated. As a full-time employee, Drucilla always dreamed of being an entrepreneur and author, and upon completing this book, she is one step closer to pursuing her dream.

CPSIA information can be obtained
at www.ICGtesting.com
Printed in the USA
FSHW012201110920

9 781662 400766